EVERY SUMMER

Claire Hennessy x

POOLBEG

Published 2009
by Poolbeg Press Ltd.
123 Grange Hill, Baldoyle,
Dublin 13, Ireland
Email: poolbeg@poolbeg.com

13 5 7 9 10 8 6 4 2

A catalogue record for this book is available from the British Library.

ISBN 978-1-84223-346-7

Typeset by Patrica Hope in Palatino 11.75/16
Printed by
CPI Cox and Wyman, Reading, RG1 8EX

www.poolbeg.com

About the author

Every Summer is Claire Hennessy's ninth book. She lives in Dublin and studied at Trinity College. Her summers are often spent writing and avoiding the sun (easy to do in Ireland). She occasionally contemplates finding more hobbies so that her author bio will be more interesting and groovy. If you wish to suggest some, or talk to her about her books, she can be found online at **www.clairehennessy.com**.

Acknowledgements

I don't know about other writery types, but I find that mostly my acknowledgements page is a sort of apology to the loved ones in one's life, who put up with living with Writer With A Book Deadline Rapidly Approaching and only occasionally try to use the 'come on, let's go party, you can use it as research!' ploy to lure one away from writing mania. So thank you, folks (you know who you are, and this sneakily saves me from embarrassment should I leave anyone out).

I am also, as ever, grateful to all at Poolbeg for being fabulous, and to those lovely, brilliant people who read, enjoy and support my books. Many, many thanks to you all.

*For my parents, Liam and Teresa, who are
very cool and wonderful people, and who cope
remarkably well with having a writer in the family.*

Prologue

She happens to be online as the messages pour in. It is a username she doesn't recognise, but of course that's the entire point, that she doesn't know exactly who it is.

She looks at what they say about her and then she starts laughing. She is probably losing her mind. It is funny, though. She doesn't know who it is. There is someone who hates her this much and she has no idea who it might be.

There is a potentially infinite shortlist of candidates for who might hate her this much. That is funny. If she doesn't laugh at it, she's going to start crying, and she's cried enough for one day.

When she's finished, when this anonymous angry person is finished with her, she logs off and goes upstairs to her bedroom to pack.

Part One

Every Summer

1

Chloe

Every summer I break someone's heart. This has been the pattern since I was eleven years old and my friend Neil tried kissing me and I laughed. I didn't mean to. When I say it like that, breaking people's hearts, it sounds intentional. It isn't. I don't set out to do it. To say that hearts get broken may be an exaggeration. I'm sure they don't, not really, even if it feels like that at the time. Boys are surprisingly emotional about some things.

Just over a year ago, two things happened in our school that made the teachers start panicking about what they call 'cyberbullying', which seems to be one of those words that only adults who have the very vaguest ideas about how the internet works actually use. This past year, we have had entire days devoted to lectures about how even though the internet can be a useful educational tool, it should also be used with caution. They talk about 'internet safety' as though it's like driving or sex or something. What they are worried about is people using certain websites, the ones that the school's internet provider blocks anyway, for making other people in the school miserable. Pages devoted to 'why Chloe Cullinane is a bitch' apparently fall into this category. I don't kid myself. I know very well that it was the Dominic stuff that was more important. Dominic was a fifth-year student who decided to post his suicide note online, which if you ask me was a cry for attention or help or something and all his friends who left farewell messages for him were rather missing the point. The school were also missing the point by obsessing over the internet aspect of things, but I suppose it's easier for them, when you have one student dead at seventeen and then, two weeks later, have the outraged stepfather of another storming in demanding an explanation for why the school haven't intervened in the 'filth' that one student has put online.

There wasn't actually anything particularly filthy about Steve's page, just a lot of incoherent swearing about why I was a whore. The pictures were Photoshopped as was obvious to anyone with a clue (which would exclude, of course, the outraged step-father – Martin still gets paranoid about paying for anything online with his credit card, convinced it will be his undoing), and it was more pathetic than anything else. I wasn't the one to point it out to Martin. It went up two days after I broke up with Steve and I could see that he was stressed – it was May, we had the Junior Cert coming up, and even though he's not particularly bright he does care about school – and I didn't worry too much about it. But Martin tries to get involved in school things – as though teaching Junior Infants makes him an expert on how teenagers are or should be educated – and knows lots of the other parents and someone pointed it out to him. And that was that. We were sent out letters over the summer and it's been a year of 'how not to use the internet'.

The real issues were two very separate things but I suppose I am glad that they haven't been focussed on. I didn't know Dominic. I probably shouldn't comment. But if you have a student who wants to kill themselves it seems to me that the important part isn't the idea of announcing it online, though the newspaper stories about the whole thing focussed a lot on the idea that 'this generation' simply don't understand reality, that we're disconnected from it. I wish they'd make up their minds. One moment we are too connected to each other, unable to go five minutes without checking the phone or the internet, the next, cut off from the world entirely.

And the real issue about me and Steve was not that he put a rant up for everyone to see, but that he was angry. I don't think I broke his heart but I think he felt it at the time. And that is what happens, what keeps happening. Not that I want to break hearts. Not that I think I am some amazingly brilliant, gorgeous, charming goddess with such tremendous power over everyone I come into contact with. But it keeps happening, this messy ending of things. Steve was the worst, I suppose, in many ways. If only because all that fuss meant we had to sit through so many talks on thoughtfulness and consideration towards one another 'even in online forums', and I couldn't roll my eyes and sigh about it being all about me because of course it wasn't, it was about Dominic, and my role in the saga was minimal – no, not minimal, but not enough, on its own, to make a difference, and just enough, after that, to make all the difference and shift the focus of his tragedy entirely. I feel guilty about that more than Steve, I think. But I can see it from their perspective. Don't talk about feelings, mental health, what it means to be depressed, what it means to call someone a whore. It is quite different to talk about these things in the context of 'internet safety'. It allows for darting around the main point and obsessing over passwords and sharing of information and being conscious of the importance of anything you say online, recorded in black-and-white (or indeed green-on-black, as Steve's thing was).

Anything you say to or about anyone is important, when it's something like 'whore'. That's indelible no matter what. For the record, I never had sex with Steve. I don't know if it matters, though. It's a word you throw out in anger and it means more than just sex. I think he meant, basically, that I was a bad person. That I was inconsiderate of him and his feelings, that I treated him badly, that I broke up with him at a bad time or without an adequate explanation. All of this is true, I suppose. That is the most damning thing of all, not that he put up badly altered images of me, but that somewhere amidst all that cursing and all those typos, he was right.

This summer, there is a Boy, not like Neil or Steve, not like Raymond, the first Steve whose friends referred to him as 'Steo', or Larry (from my summers at twelve, thirteen and fourteen, respectively), but a Boy who I can nevertheless tell you, right now, that I do not Love-with-a-capital-L.

And even though it is only barely June I can tell you that I am asking myself already: if you don't love them, well, what's the point?

2

Lynn

Every summer since I was about seven has been spent hopping from one summer programme to another, always on the go, doing something. I have spent weeks at a time immersed in Irish, French, Spanish, music, art, drama. We go away for two weeks and that's it, then, the summer gone, with only a few days here and there of just being at home and appreciating that it's summer. Summer is always busy, scheduled. This is probably why, when Jennifer-Next-Door asks me what I'm up to this summer, she looks surprised when I say, "Oh, you know, just hanging around here".

Not the right thing to say.

"Hanging around? Ah, that doesn't sound like you. You must have loads going on."

Jennifer-Next-Door is right. It isn't like me. She is also fishing for information here. What am I up to this summer and how can she praise me for it in a way that will somehow inevitably compare me unfavourably to her daughter?

I laugh. "Ah, you know yourself." Meaningless. Totally meaningless. And then I nod and wave and duck into the house before she has time to probe further into what I might be doing from now until the end of August.

Dad's home, Mum's working. He's a photographer, she's a yoga teacher. Neither of them work normal nine-to-five-ish hours and figuring out whether you can count on either of them to be around at a given time is headache-inducing, particularly as Dad's schedule is all over the place and Mum's, though a little more stable, includes random things like giving talks which tend to have phrases like 'finding yourself' in the title. You would think she would be self-aware. You would also think that someone like Dad who is paid to find and record the beauty in a particular scene, or capture the special moments of people's lives, would be above the ridiculous competition with Jennifer-Next-Door. You would be wrong about that.

"I was just talking to Jennifer," I tell him, because she will mention it the next time she sees him.

He nods, looks up from the sauce he's stirring on the hob. "You know Sheila's going away soon."

"Yeah, I know," I say. She's going away to the States, some leadership conference thing, something exciting and elite and expensive that looks very impressive on a CV. She's the only one from our school going.

"It's a great opportunity for her," he says.

"Yeah, I know," I say again.

"Would you ever want to do something like that?" he asks. "I mean, it's probably too late for this year, but next year, maybe. If you wanted to."

"It's not really my thing," I say, and then I say what I think might put an end to this. "I don't know if it's as great as it looks, I think a lot of people just go for the sake of the trip and meeting people, you know?"

"Oh, of course, of course. But still, Jennifer was saying it seems to look really interesting . . ."

"If you're interested in that sort of thing. I'm not," I say firmly. "I'm not Sheila, stop comparing the two of us, for God's sake." Not annoyed. Just – okay, a little annoyed.

Dad laughs. "I'm not comparing anyone. I was just saying it looked like a great opportunity for her."

Ridiculous. Absolutely ridiculous. Mum and Dad and Jennifer-and-David-Next-Door have been doing

12

this for years and they always deny it as though it isn't patently obvious.

"Occasionally we do discuss our children, you know," he continues, chuckling. "Dinner's at six."

Sheila is the same age as me. I'm seventeen in September, her birthday is in October. I neither like nor dislike her. She is not a huge part of my life, even though we go to the same school. Most of the time when we talk it's about our parents and what they say to one another and what they say to us about each other, which means that for most of our lives we've known all too well that my parents wish I was more like Sheila and her parents wish she was more like me. It's okay as long as it's even. This is the summer I think it might not be. That's maybe why I want to shout at Dad for not admitting what's actually going on, but the older I get the more I have to conclude it has to do with a lack of self-awareness. Mum too. There is a certain irony to getting stressed out about having to give talks in which terms like 'inner peace' heavily feature.

Adults would rather not have their flaws pointed out to them, particularly by their own children. I am rising above it.

This summer I have another few days left as an exam attendant and that's it as far as work plans go. And apart from the occasional music festival towards the end of the summer, there isn't much planned in terms of fun either. No family holiday because we can't find a time that suits everyone (i.e. Mum and Dad). No holiday with my friends because they're all either going away with their families or with other sets of friends. Sheila-Next-Door has yet to go on a holiday with her friends and without adult supervision so it's unlikely they'd let me go, anyway. No brushing up on language skills, no taking classes in something I'm not overly into. And no orchestra, which is something they verbally recognise as my choice but are also worried that I'll regret later. I'm doing music in school, it's not like I'm going to forget everything I've ever learned.

I don't regret it. I won't.

This summer is not going to be like the other summers. I just haven't figured out how, exactly, I am going to make it as worthwhile as all the others in its own way. Or even if it needs to be.

My phone rings and I answer with, "Oh, come on, I *just* said goodbye to you, aren't you sick of me yet?"

He laughs. "Not possible."

And even though I know it's an immensely stupid situation to let myself be in, I melt.

3

Alice

Every summer I pretend or maybe really do believe it for a while: this will be the summer when I change, when I emerge from the chrysalis a beautiful butterfly. My hair will be golden and luxurious, my skin flawless and lightly tanned (just enough to look healthy, but nowhere near as orange as to invite comparisons with the fake-tan Oompa-Loompa look), my figure slender but discernibly feminine, my legs long, my smile radiant. I will be able to walk in high heels without wobbling like a little girl playing dress-up. I will be able to toss my hair over my shoulder and smile mysteriously yet interestingly. I will fascinate people who don't know me, the way Chloe does. Maybe not quite as enigmatic as Chloe. A little more accessible. I will be friendly, charming. I will tell jokes and people will laugh at them and I will remember the punch line instead of trailing off helplessly or giggling before delivering it and ruining the entire thing.

Summer is magical; that enchanted period in between school years, where you can reinvent yourself. It must be possible. Three months where, if you're me, you only see a handful of the people you have to spend the rest of the year seeing too much of. I want to be that girl who returns to school as someone who has finally blossomed. The swan.

The first time the fantasy occurred to me I was ten. Maybe I'd been watching too many makeover television programmes, or too many of those films where the already-beautiful girl takes her hair down or takes off her glasses or something and is suddenly utterly irresistible to all the boys around her. I had one of those from-afar crushes on this boy called Brian in my class at school, who of course knew I existed but who would never think to speak to me or think about me or be interested in me the way he was interested in the girls he hung around with at break time. He'd kissed at least two of them, and had briefly had a girlfriend who was eleven and in the year above us. Even now it's a big deal for a girl to have a boyfriend a whole year younger than she

16

is, never mind back then. Boys have to be particularly impressive for the girl to escape criticism.

I decided I was crazy about him because he was good-looking and charming – no, I didn't decide, I just was. I just was and I couldn't help myself, only I was just ordinary boring Alice, not deserving of his attention or of being looked at as though I was worthy of it. Talking to him or trying to be his friend was out of the question. It has always been. There are some girls who can do that. Lynn. God. I didn't know her in primary school, but she would probably, if I told her this story, laugh and ask me why I didn't just *ask* him if he liked me. If I had been Lynn maybe I would have, because if I had been Lynn he would have at least seen me.

It's not that she's stunningly beautiful. Jack once called her fat – not to her face, thankfully – and I was horrified by this. She's not that either. He can be overly critical at times, especially considering he's not even interested in girls. Lynn is I suppose what people would call curvy, not skinny but not overweight, blessed with hips and breasts and a grown-up-ness about her that I can't link to one particular physical characteristic. It's her attitude as well. She is a woman when the rest of us are still girls. I can imagine her at ten, hands on her hips, asking Brian, "Well, do you like me or not?" And he'd look at her and at the very least, even at that age, be impressed that she had the guts to ask him. Even if he said no, she'd shrug her shoulders and declare that, well, that was that then.

And if it had been Chloe, he would have liked her already, probably. He would have gazed at her perfection – and oh, I know Chloe isn't perfect. It is impossible to think that your friends are perfect. But she is beautiful, in a quiet sort of way, in the way that once you look at her you keep looking and she just seems to get more attractive every time. She's Snow White, without the dwarves and the singing, all black hair and fair skin and red lips (redness aided, since she was fourteen, with lipstick, but apart from that she can do without make-up – it's as though the acne demon was so charmed by her that he decided to forgo cursing her like the rest of us). There are not enough words in the universe to accurately convey how much, at one point in my life, I wanted to look like Chloe, to step inside her skin.

But I can't turn into Chloe over a summer, or ever. She's tiny, delicate, the sort of creature I imagine boys feel protective of. (Jack tells me this is a myth, this idea that all boys want to be the protector all the time. I am once again ignoring him on the grounds of gayness. When I want to delve into the complicated psyche of the young gay male in Dublin today my big brother will be the first one I turn to.) And Chloe attracts so many boys that using clichés as explanations seems justified. People want to take care of her, to stand up for her. Last year in school, right before we did our Junior Cert, one of her ex-boyfriends posted a lot of really horrible stuff about her online, and another guy apparently – all right, I don't know if this is true, but it sounds like the sort of thing that tends to happen where Chloe is involved – beat him up for it. Thumpings after school are hardly the stuff of chivalric romance but it's something, in this day and age, to inspire that kind of thing.

I am pale and uninteresting. I don't have that dramatic contrast of fair and dark the way Chloe does, or the confident red curls that you'd never dream of labelling as ginger when they're bouncing on Lynn's shoulders. Wispy dark-blonde hair, the kind I could dye a lighter, brighter shade if it wasn't for the risk of destroying my hair entirely. (Finally some useful advice from Jack, which seemed a bit of a cliché; I squinted at him for a moment and wondered if he was in danger of morphing from my big brother into a flamboyantly camp hairdresser but the notion soon passed.) I am thin in a way that makes people jealous except it's not in an attractive way; I just look like a taller and much spottier version of myself at ten or eleven. I'm going to be seventeen and I don't look it. I am always the one, even though it's Chloe who's tiny, to be turned away from clubs when there are bouncers at the door, who is asked for ID, who worries that everyone is going to be not let in somewhere or kicked out of somewhere because I don't look any-where close to adulthood.

Every summer I dream that this will be it. This will be the summer I will be able to go to the beach without feeling as though I might as well have worn a kid's one-piece swimsuit because my bikini top doesn't have all that much to hide. This will be the summer I transform into someone who looks recognisably teenage, almost womanly, someone beautiful or at least on her way to being there. When I saunter back into school on August 26 – it will have to be a saunter, no other way of walking will do – people will look at me and marvel at what the summer has done for me. My skin will be clear and I will look people in the eye and the summer will have done its work and all its possibilities will have been realised.

It's still June. Maybe I'm still hoping, a little bit, even at nearly-seventeen: this summer, this will be it.

4

Lynn

Being an exam attendant is generally regarded as a cushy job and rightly so. It's well-paid considering it's only for a couple of weeks and all you're doing is escorting nervous examinees to the toilets, minding mobile phones, and bringing in tea, coffee, and biscuits to the supervisors halfway through each exam. You'd think I'd feel guiltier about that. Junior Cert last summer, Leaving Cert next summer – you'd think I'd be more sympathetic to the students, who are the ones who might actually benefit from a caffeine jolt midway through the paper. But I get it, now. We don't have much to do, and neither do the supervisors. We have to figure out ways of filling the time.

I've been reading and bringing my iPod with me religiously. We're not supposed to have them, really, but as long as you don't have the volume up so high everyone can hear it, it's fine. It is, as Mrs O'Brien put it to us, only the responsible fifth-years who are entrusted with this task of ensuring that – well, that the supervisors get their tea and coffee, I suppose. We have no real power. No instructions as to what to do if someone is found with notes in the toilets, or a promise of extra cash if we find someone cheating. Alice was convinced that it was true, that you got some kind of bonus if you did. But that's Alice for you.

Six of us here, one per exam centre – classroom, really, filled with stressed-out sixth-years – and another bunch upstairs with the Junior Certs. All of us responsible fifth-years. Most of them I still don't know very well. With Transition Year being optional, fifth year is a mix of people who've done it and people who haven't, so if you skip it, as I did, you find yourself mixed in with the year above you, the ones you've never had any reason to get to know. By fifth year, making new friends is extra effort. Not worth it in most cases.

And then there was Neil.

Neil is the reason I'm here, even though it is the sort of bits-and-pieces endeavour more suitable for one who has something else going on this summer, rather than someone who doesn't know what she's doing beyond Friday. The last week of exams there are only a couple of centres open, because all the 'big' exams are over and done with, so we're out of here. We go for lunch together, make the trip down to the staffroom to get the tea and coffee together, and hang out in the evenings. He should be sick of me at this point. The evenings are what surprise me. This was a way of making sure I'd still see him even though we weren't in school together all day – by, essentially, ensuring that we got another week and a half of being in school together, all day. But, like sitting through classes together, it's a low-level sort of friendship. You need the evenings to talk properly. We can't spend all day chatting when we're supposed to be quiet, and it's ridiculous to be texting someone constantly when they're sitting at a desk just down the corridor from you. This didn't stop us from spending last Thursday sending messages about the others here, inventing ludicrous back-stories for them that made it difficult not to burst out into giggles every few minutes. We are not all friends here. The others mostly dismiss us. Some of them think we're a couple.

I don't obsess over what other people think of me, but that part I like. Couple. Lynn and Neil.

Neillynn, the names slide easily together. We are not, of course. Never will be.

Suddenly there's a chin resting on my shoulder, making me jump. I turn around and of course it's him. There's no-one else here who would dream of getting that close.

Down to the staffroom to start the water boiling, to contemplate which kind of biscuits to set out on a nice paper doily today. They tend to be dull and plain, because of potential nut allergies. I find the song on my iPod that I want Neil to listen to, and he takes one earpiece and I take the other and we dance.

There's nothing quite like dancing to the music that only two of you can hear. He dances badly. It's a well-worn joke at this point that he can't actually be gay if his sense of rhythm is that atrocious. But he's enthusiastic.

And I love to dance. I don't have the figure for ballet or the patience for anything with complicated steps but I love it all the same. It's the part of me that is most like my mum, I think. She stretches and contorts herself into yoga poses, only she stays there, calm, Zen, breathing deeply. But when she moves through them quickly, doing the sun salute or whatever it's called, it's like dancing. Moving your body in a way that on the one hand is fixed, there

24

are only so many things you can do with it, and on the other hand is all yours. Your body, your choice of moves. When you dance you rarely do something original, but it is still yours. Your response to the music, to the situation.

There's that saying about how you should dance like nobody's watching. Having somebody watching is sometimes what you need, if it's someone who's grinning, watching you, cheering you on, appreciating you, admiring you. Even if you know it's not romantic. Even if you know they're never going to be tempted to lean over and dip you back and kiss you.

So we dance, the two of us, as the water boils, needing to stay close so that the earpieces stay in our ears. Not quite like nobody's watching. We're still at it, onto the next song on the playlist, when two of the girls who are attendants for the Junior Cert come in to sort out their own biscuits and tea. Marie and Georgina, they're in our chemistry class. Neil and I are lab partners. An obvious joke there that got us through most of the first term. We have chemistry together, nudge nudge wink wink. By summer term it had morphed into comments like, "And after lunch, it's off to bed, will you bring the handcuffs or should I?"

"Excuse me," Marie says with the tired air of one who has spent her entire morning asking dancing teenagers to stop getting in the way of the biscuit cupboard, instead of ploughing through whatever dense tome she's brought with her today. Marie is also in our English class. Very intellectual. Sort of the Sheila-Next-Door of this year.

"Sorry," I say.

"Sorry," Neil says.

We step back. Try not to giggle. Around Neil I'm a giggler. It's not just that he's funny. Around him, I'm funnier. Things are funnier. There's more laughter in the world.

Have you ever met someone like that, someone who just – oh dear, here we go with the clichés – brightens things?

If I were even more like my mum I'd say he's a bundle of positive energy or something like that. But I'm not. So I won't.

Tempting, though.

5

Alice

Oh don't look at me, please don't look at me, please don't see me.

On the other hand, do, please, yes, come and sit with me, come and talk to me, come and be my friend.

The dilemma, when sitting upstairs on the bus into town and seeing a co-worker getting on, is whether to pose so that it looks like you're gazing out the window, lost in contemplation, or to attempt to time your glancing around at the passengers going up the stairs in such a way that she sees you, catches your eye, and sits next to you.

I can't keep watching the passengers getting on. That makes it look as though I'm waiting for her, like I'm some sort of crazy stalker who thinks we're best friends forever. And she probably won't want to sit next to me. So I try to look as though I am staring into space and lost in a reverie and not frozen into position by the knowledge that she's going to be able to see me any moment now.

It is a relief and a loss when the bus moves off again without any additions to my seat. Maybe she hasn't seen me, which means that we don't need to make awkward conversation for the rest of the journey. Or maybe she has, and decided not to sit next to me because, oh that Alice girl is so boring or clueless or otherwise unworthy of her time and energy.

Someday, when I am a grown-up, I will be able to travel to and from work without panicking about whether or not the girls I work with will talk to me or like me. I will chat easily to them and be a part of things and when the new girls start work they will marvel at me, look up to me.

As we get closer to the city centre I contemplate getting off one stop earlier, to avoid awkward conversations about neither of us knowing we got this bus and where we live, but then she does so I don't have to, and I wonder if it's deliberate or not. If Gemma in all her eighteen-year-old perfection and glory actually has somewhere else to pop into before work, or if she is avoiding me. Am I really so painful to talk to that people need to take such measures? God, it's possible, it's entirely possible.

I practise my bright face, bright smile as I walk to the shop in the not-quite-summery morning sunshine. The customer is always right, smile smile smile, except that half the time they will be trying to steal something so for God's sake don't let them out of your sight.

For the rest of the summer, three days a week most weeks and then some Sundays as well, depending on how they're fixed I suppose, I am working in one of the kind of glittery accessories shop that I loved when I was thirteen and still feel a little like I should be in awe of. The fact that they're letting me work here. Wow.

It's been almost two weeks. I got the job at the end of May, a week after saying goodbye to Transition Year and feeling sorry for people like Lynn who still had exams to sit. I suppose it's still too early for all of us to be Best Friends Forever even though the other girls seem to click in a way that I don't get, and some of them have only just started too. It's as though they have a common language, one that sounds like English to the untrained ear, but when I try to speak it I fail miserably at it.

We sell overpriced earrings, belly-button rings, toe-rings, nose-rings, every kind of ring you can think of. Necklaces and bracelets and anklets, fake tattoos and skimpy underwear and faux-silk scarves, an insane number of objects to put in your hair (I still haven't figured out exactly how to use half of them, though by the end of the summer I hope to have established what they're all for and how you'd wear them, and be the kind of girl who has a wider choice beyond the tried-and-tested ponytail even with the hopeless hair that I have been cursed with). It is assumed we know what everything is actually *for*. I live in fear of a customer, or indeed my supervisor, finding me out.

This morning I'm on the floor. Customer-stalking. This is the part of the job I hate. I'm not good at being pushy. I can't do it without it being obvious. Gemma, now, Gemma is amazing. She chats to the customers, bright and smiley, teeth showing. She asks them if they're buying something for themselves, for a special occasion, as a gift, and then offers them advice in a way that lets them think they've come up with the idea themselves. I am always horribly aware that I'm trying to trick them into buying something else. There is no official sales quota, but unofficially it is the kind of thing that can get you fired under the guise of not providing appropriate customer service or something like that (as I have picked up from snippets of conversation).

It is about an hour in when I become conscious of the way my supervisor has picked up on my tendency to let Gemma do the customer-stalking and to instead busy myself with straightening displays and ensuring scarves and hats are firmly on their hangers. The next customer. I'll take the next one, I vow.

Two minutes of browsing. That is what they're allowed before we pounce. Two minutes before we step in with a bright, cheery, "Hi, can I help you? Are you looking for anything in particular?"

The girl turns around. "Oh my God, Alice! I didn't know you were working here!"

Shelley. Eoin's little sister. Two years behind me in school and about five years ahead of me in the real world. She's already adequately accessorised. We sell those earrings, that belt, and everything else looks like the kind of item you'd find in a glossy magazine. Stylish. Now. This is adolescence in the twenty-first century and it is glamorous.

How on earth did I ever impress Eoin when this is his most immediate model for what teenage girls are?

"Um, yeah," I say. "Yeah, I, ah, started a couple of weeks ago, it's – how are you?"

What I mean is, how's Eoin, who I haven't seen since school finished and who I haven't spoken to properly for much longer.

"Great, yeah! I'm soooo glad school's over, I couldn't wait to get out of there."

"How were your exams?" I ask, and then realise it's a stupid question. Shelley looks as though she's forgotten she ever had them. Not everyone cares about school exams, I remind myself. What a thing to talk about, to ask about. I'm like those elderly relatives who pinch your cheek and ask you what year you're in at school now and tell you how like your mother you're getting.

"Ah, yeah, grand, whatever, they're done – you didn't have any, right? Lucky. Can't wait to do Transition Year, you don't seem to do anything, must be brilliant."

"Yeah, it is," I say, half-heartedly. How's Eoin? How's Eoin?

"Like, Eoin didn't even bother going in half the time," she continues.

An exaggeration. One third of the time, maybe. But here we are at my favourite destination: talking about him.

"Yeah, I know, I haven't –"

"Oh my God," she interrupts, "isn't this gorgeous?" She picks up a necklace and holds it up against her already-decorated throat, peering in the mirror.

Deliberate or not? I don't know. I wonder.

My supervisor's watching me, possibly about to

give out to me as soon as Shelley leaves because we're not supposed to hang around chatting to friends.

"It is," I say. "It really suits you."

"You think?" she says, looking at me as though she genuinely cares what I have to say, as though I'm some kind of oracle.

"Yeah, the colour . . ." I trail off there. I have always found it difficult to give compliments to people, even when I mean it. But my inarticulacy doesn't seem to bother her. Maybe she just wanted someone to agree with her.

She ends up buying the necklace and the bracelet that goes with it. A good sale. She skips off and I still have no idea what Eoin might be doing for the summer.

6

Chloe

The Boy, in what I can only assume is an attempt to be sensitive, caring and the sort of boy I want, has a habit of asking me questions when there are better things we could be doing. We're in his bedroom, door closed, curtains pulled over, no adults at home. His parents are at work. So are Mam and Martin, for that matter, but Martin's days are short and he'll be back home with Patrick soon.

Sometimes I wonder if what Mam was looking for was an unpaid babysitter, when she started going out with him. I suppose that's unfair, to look at it that way. They've been together for nearly six years now. Parents for four and a half years – I don't kid myself, I know very well that Patrick is what makes them parents-together. I would never have been enough. They got married two years ago. Marrying the men she has kids with is apparently not much of a priority for Mam.

And that again is unfair. She was never going to marry my dad, who is a blurry figure in my imagination and who I have never met in real life. She was maybe – probably – always going to marry Martin. She just wanted to do it properly and apparently you can't plan weddings overnight. I wouldn't know. I can't imagine ever doing it. Even if you love someone how can you be sure you'll still love them in a year, in ten, in twenty?

The Boy asks me questions when we're in bed together. Dressed, still, but dressed in summer clothes, him in shorts and me in a floaty green dress, and our bare legs touching. I am kissing his neck and he's asking me about my family, what they're like, if we get along, if they understand me.

What I want to say is something cold. We're not going to discuss this, I could say, and get up and walk out. As though there is anything dramatic about my family, when there isn't. I will not moan about my stable two-parent family and an adorable younger brother and any minor grievances. Not to him and not to anyone.

Instead I change the direction. "Do yours understand you?" I ask, looking into his eyes.

He laughs. "Yeah, right. They don't have a clue. My dad, right, he's all . . ."

I'm trying to care. I really am. I nod and look sympathetic at all the right moments. He doesn't get on with his dad. That's about it. Like every sixteen-year-old boy in the world, he doesn't get on with his dad, and they disagree over how he should be spending his time or what he should be working towards in school or who his friends are. It is a tale of many specific, mundane incidents.

"And then he actually slams the door and says that I need to 'sort out' my attitude, me, like, when he's practically about to beat the shit out of me . . ."

If I loved him, if I was even infatuated with him, I would find it all riveting. I would think him unique and special, and his problems even more so. I wouldn't be able to see how silly it all is. I would be gazing reverently at him and admiring his bravery and perseverance instead of thinking less of him for being so whiny.

I want so badly to be the kind of good person who will listen and care. I am good at listening. It means not having to talk about yourself. It is the caring, the genuine, honest caring, that I have trouble with.

The easy part is stroking his hair. Resting my head on his shoulder. Moving my fingertips along his forearms. It's the simple and exquisite touching of another person, of being next to them, close to them. This is the part I can do and have it be entirely truthful.

This is the part I want to last forever, the part after the talking and before the inevitable sex. The quiet intimacy where it doesn't matter that he is just an ordinary boy who thinks the world is out to get him, because he's here with me and I'm here with him and despite it all I feel safe and peaceful in a way that I can't explain except that maybe it doesn't matter whose arms you have around you as long as they are someone's.

7

Lynn

On my last day of 'attending', my supervisor counts out the twenties for me and thanks me for all my hard work. Grown-up work-small-talk nonsense. She neither means it nor doesn't mean it. She's probably not even listening to what she's saying.

I've expected that this will feel like it's now properly the summer holidays, walking out of school today, except it's raining as heavily as any day in winter.

"So," I say to Neil, "still on for tomorrow?"

"Yeah!" he says, full of enthusiasm. "You have to make sure I have positive memories to cling to when I'm out in the wilderness."

"So that when you're trekking across the desert, like . . ."

"Yeah, exactly. I'm going to need something to give me hope." He stops, and puts his hands on my shoulders, and looks at me seriously. "Lynn Delaney, are you ready to take on this responsibility?"

"I think I'm up to it, sir," I say.

"You'd better be," he responds solemnly, and then we crack up.

And he takes his hands off my shoulders and we keep walking.

I order myself not to obsess over this moment later, the moment of hope that inevitably comes from standing that close to a beautiful boy in the rain.

"I don't know what I'm going to do without you," I muse, making it sound casual.

"You will have trouble coping," he nods. "I don't know how you're going to manage it."

"Support groups."

"Alcoholism. I know it's got a bad name for itself but, look, if it gets you through those cold empty nights . . ."

"I'll have a think about it." And here we are at the corner where we go our separate ways.

He hugs me. "See you tomorrow."

"Yeah, yeah, I suppose you will," I reply, and walk the rest of the way home biting my lip happily. Absurd. Insane. The whole thing.

On Sunday he's going off into the middle of

nowhere, or rather some boarding school in the middle of nowhere for French college. His parents want him to brush up on his language skills before next year. Three weeks of language immersion. I've done it for Spanish and couldn't take it seriously. It's so artificial. Irish college I get. The part of the real world you're going to for those few weeks actually speaks the language at least some of the time.

Of course when I went to France, four weeks out of the summer before the Junior Cert, two years ago now, everyone apart from the family I was staying with nodded politely at my initial attempts and then replied to me in English, as if to say, please, for the love of God, stop butchering our glorious language. So Neil will probably end up learning more than I did during his sojourn out in 'the wilderness'.

I decide to buy him a beret. That'll make him laugh.

I'm hopeless. I know this, I know this, and I can't fix it.

8

Alice

"Hey, honey, how was work?" Mum asks.

"Great," I say, big smile, and then remember that I'm at home and I don't have to sell things anymore. I sigh, the sigh of being able to sit down for the rest of the day and lie on the couch and watch television and not have to be fake-happy for another day and a half. I wonder how people manage to work full-time, to do this kind of work full-time especially. It's wearing me out.

"It was okay," I add. "Tiring."

"On your feet all day?" she asks.

I nod, and she looks sympathetic. But it's the wrong thing to be sympathetic about. My feet are fine. (My feet are actually not fine. They are ugly

41

and my toes are too long and my toenails are not perfectly painted and most of the other girls have taken to wearing open-toe shoes on days with a hint of sunshine and I feel completely out of my depth. I never think about my toes except for at the beach, and even then that's only a few days, really, and you can prepare for that. These girls must paint their toenails and shave their legs and have their bodies constantly ready for the opportunity to show off any part of it. Like superheroes, perpetually poised to rip off their clothing and leap into action. So my feet are not fine. But they're not the issue.)

Sometimes I am not entirely sure how I got the job. The interview was very formal, very much about trotting out the stock responses that we have been taught in school. (Transition Year is filled with careers workshops. We had to do a practice interview at one point, which terrified me. The real one was easier.) I felt wooden, as though I was just reading out loud in class, monotonous and predictable. They – there were two of them asking me questions – told me afterwards I seemed very professional. I professionally thanked them and left. I thought they were making fun of me, being patronising. It felt like a pat on the head, a thanks-for-trying, you're cute, but we can't possibly let you work in this environment where you need to be pretty and bubbly.

"Do you want tea?" Mum calls after me, as I plod up the stairs to take off my make-up and shoes and work clothes.

"Yes, please!" And within five minutes I'm on the couch, in my dressing-gown and with a clean if not beautiful face. I can feel an angry red lump on my chin, one which will probably take ages to disappear entirely.

"Stop poking at it," Mum says almost automatically as she sets a cup of tea in front of me.

"I'm not," I say, just as automatically. I can't remember how often we have had conversations like this over the past however many years it has been. It is a depressing saga: Alice's Bad Skin Years.

"We could do one of those home facial things this weekend," she suggests. Oh bless her, she does try.

"Mmmm," I say, vaguely, picking up the remote control. "Do you want to watch something?" Can we get away from this topic, please?

She sits down, and I click my way up the channels until we find something to watch.

"Are we still going ahead with the barbecue?" she asks at the break.

"Oh, yeah, I suppose so," I say. I hadn't thought about it, really. Next weekend is my birthday. Seventeen. In primary school I used to have birthday parties. Everyone went to everyone else's birthday party, and you handed out invitations and then people almost had to go and it was a big deal not to invite someone. Since secondary school started, my birthdays have always been in the summer holidays, and everyone's away. Or possibly still around and I just don't know it. Apart from Shelley, who hardly qualifies as a friend, and Jodie, who works in the local bookshop, I haven't seen anyone from school since it ended.

I make a mental list of people to invite. Lynn. Maybe she'll want to bring that guy Neil. She is just the teensiest bit in love with him. I don't know him that well. I wonder if he'd secretly judge me for not having loads of people there. Chloe. Chloe may want to bring Gordon – or did she break up with him? I try to remember. Chloe doesn't make announcements about the ending or for that matter the beginning of her relationships. Some girls never shut up about their boyfriends. With Chloe, getting anything out of her is like pulling teeth.

Jodie. I can invite Jodie, and Donna if she's around and not on holidays somewhere, and then that's it. That's it.

Sometimes I really miss Eoin, not just for his Eoin-ness but for the way I got to be friendly with a whole lot of other people from school who I'd known for ages but had never seen outside of school. For a brief period of time I was Eoin's Girlfriend and suddenly magically worth talking to. But when people are really your boyfriend's friends, and you only go out together for a couple of months, they quickly return to being just his friends. I'm right back where I started.

Someday I would like to be in the position where I can run into them somewhere and smile at them vaguely as though I think I might remember them but they're not important enough to remember properly or important enough to acknowledge the fact that we once spent hours talking about the careers of Irish comedians in the UK or why the original Power Rangers were much cooler than the later ones. I will look at them the way they looked at me when we had our big end-of-Transition-Year ceremony in school, as though I no longer register as someone they know and are friendly with. And then I will nod at Eoin, and walk out of the room leaving him wistful and regretting that he ever broke up with me, because no one has ever quite managed to live up to me.

He will wish that he could turn back time, and when he runs after me I will sigh and shake my head and tell him that it's too late, and then go off to have some kind of fabulous life.

In this version of reality, the barbecue will be

attended by more people than my immediate family and a couple of friends. And I will have better skin and painted toenails. And I will spend less time daydreaming, because I won't need to. I will be happy.

9

Lynn

On my quest to find a beret for Neil, I go into the shop where Alice works. I'm still glancing around, seeing if she's working today, when a tall blonde creature approaches me with a fake smile and says, "Hi there, are you looking for something in particular?"

It's that kind of shop. I see. My usual response is to ignore these people.

"Do you have any berets?" I ask.

The blonde creature frowns. "Um."

"Black, pretentious, French," I elaborate, and then, not entirely sure why I do this, because it's not like I have anything to prove to this random girl, add, "It's for my boyfriend."

It's amazing how her face changes, from looking

vaguely bewildered to genuinely smiling. "Awwww," she says. "Let me just check with one of the other girls, okay?"

When she returns, she announces, "Okay. So we've got something in a kind of brown, or there's a place down the road that might be better, if . . ."

I opt for the place down the road. She beams at me as I leave, hoping that my boyfriend likes the hat.

I don't know why I said boyfriend.

I don't know why I am shopping for a present for someone I barely knew a year ago. Our school is not a tiny place. It's entirely possible to be in the same year as someone and not know much about them other than to recognise their name and face, and then suddenly end up sitting next to them when you find yourself in a class that seems to be mostly filled with strangers, kids from the year ahead of you. You seek out a familiar face and then there one is, and you just click, right away, and you're making each other laugh by the end of the day. Some friendships happen quickly.

Most summers, I half-forget about school friendships. Not Alice, and not Sheila-Next-Door even though she hardly counts as an actual friend, but the others. This year most of them did Transition Year and I didn't see that much of them even when we were all in school, so it's not surprising that I haven't seen them since it ended. I wasn't really thinking too much about friends when I decided not to go through the motions for getting into Transition Year. They make you write an essay about what you think you'll get out of the experience and why you want to do it, but at the end of the day they're not looking for anything spectacular, just a way of deciding how to divide up the year. The ones that end up going straight into fifth year are a curious mix of people who don't want to waste time saving the planet or whatever it is one does that year and instead get straight back into another exam cycle, and people who wouldn't have minded doing TY because of general laziness, but whose general laziness meant they didn't bother writing the essay. I just want to get out of school faster. Another year and I'm finished.

I can see already that most of the school friendships won't last beyond school. Sometimes people are only friends because they have to spend so much time together. So many times during the summer, at Irish college or on a drama course or whatever it might be, I've met people and we've got really close, only to have it fade as soon as the summer ends. I have a whole bunch of people who I only communicate with online, when we're bored, even though some of them live close enough to organise regular reunions. You just stop having enough in common with people. Time passes.

And then there are the ones that you do keep in touch with, and who are still friends despite it being an effort. Diane keeps me up-to-date with all the orchestra scandal, the ongoing adventures of these people who are delighted I'm not around anymore, even though I used to think she was one of them. Simon still extends invitations to house parties to me, and we still have something to talk about when I do go, even though it's been three years since we were put in the same group for improvisation. But mostly it all fades away, and you're left with hardly anything.

This usually isn't a problem when you've an entire summer of courses and classes and camps planned. Usually I'm kept busy. Making new friends all over the place. Doing things.

He likes the beret. When I give it to him that evening, he is delighted, kissing me on both cheeks, and we fling ourselves on the couch for our last night together before he leaves.

"Don't go," I say over-dramatically when it's time for me to go home.

"I must, my dear, I must," he replies.

"Just – don't forget me," I say.

"I could never forget you, my dear!"

"Love you."

"Love you too. Now off to bed with you."

10

Chloe

Unquestionably it makes me a bad friend and a bad person to get a text message from Alice and realise firstly that I haven't spoken to her in almost a month and secondly that I don't really want to go to this barbecue.

She has added 'bring your current beau if you want!' with a smiley face at the end, which I can't look at.

I don't tell the Boy, because he will not be going. I must, I suppose. Alice is my best friend, if we still have such things at our age. I am not sure if I am hers. When I say best friend I don't mean that we share all our secrets and have sleepovers every weekend and text each other every second of every day. But out of everyone at school, the girls at least, she is the one I actually consider a real friend. She's not the sort who will bitch about you behind your back, which is something. Most of the girls in school don't like me. This isn't to do with the Steve thing, as far as I can tell. The Steve thing was more a catalyst, an excuse for them to say openly everything they'd already been thinking, to give their own reasons for 'why Chloe Cullinane is a bitch'.

Alice is the sort of person that makes you want to be a better person, if only because she is just so hopelessly innocent about some things. There was this party when we were in second year, a party at the end of the school year that one of the girls had in her house, this place with a huge back garden and a tree-house and swings. I went with this guy Larry and we spent most of our time in that tree-house. The girl, Erica, deliberately didn't invite Alice or Lynn, even though technically they were supposed to be her friends. Because Alice is sometimes awkward and Lynn is a bit of a know-it-all, and I could see the reasons even if I still thought it was a bit mean. And a few weeks after we came back to school that autumn, there were a bunch of people talking about something that had happened in the party, and it became horribly obvious all of a sudden that everyone had been there except for Lynn and Alice. And Lynn knew, straight away. I could tell from the way she pursed her lips and then gave Erica this cold look but said nothing, that she knew. But Alice just looked around wide-eyed and then Erica said something stupid, like, 'Yeah, Alice, you never got back to me on that – were you away or something then?'

Alice smiled now that it was all cleared up, and on the conversation went, and I wasn't sure whether I wanted to shake her or hug her.

I know I will go to this barbecue, not because I think it will be spectacularly fun, but because of that. And because when everyone was muttering knowingly all the way through our talks on 'internet safety' this year, she used to turn to me and smile brightly and start chatting about something inconsequential. Because I owe her.

I am a bad friend and a bad person but this at least I will do. It's the least I can do.

Part Two

The First Boy

11

Alice

The first boyfriend I ever had was Eoin. It is embarrassing to be turning seventeen and only having had one boyfriend in your entire life, though more embarrassing to be sixteen and never having had a boyfriend ever.

Some girls not only have a whole list of boyfriends but a litany of boys they've been with, the boys they've kissed at discos or parties or on drunken nights in the park. They exchange certain glances with their friends the next week in class when the teacher moves people around to stop them from talking to their friends all the time and they end up next to some guy they kissed but now regret.

It's hard to keep up with it sometimes. Some girls

assume you know the whole story already. I never know whether this is self-absorption and thinking that the world revolves around them and that everyone has been talking about it all anyway, or just being aware that people often really have been talking about it anyway because it's more interesting than whatever the teachers are talking about. And it's something, to feel as though someone feels you're enough a part of things to know what they're talking about.

I don't go out a lot, which is the sort of thing which bothers me in the abstract more than anything else. It is stressful, the whole business. Every time I pretend that it will be fun and that I am the kind of girl who can talk to people without getting flustered. Or that I am even the kind of girl that people will notice. I have sat in parks with groups from school, almost invisible. I have made excuses and minded coats and bags while people dance as though it's the easiest thing in the world to do, as though their bodies are their friends.

I think house parties might be my way forward, that right mix of social and comfortable. Even if I don't turn into a beautiful swan I can sit and talk to people sometimes, find a quiet corner somewhere and talk as though we are the only two people in the world. That was how it was with Eoin.

It was Donna's birthday, back in February, and

Donna was my best friend in primary school and still invites me to these things, and Lynn had some orchestra thing so I was there mostly on my own. I say mostly because Chloe was there too, but she'd vanished off somewhere, and I was talking to Donna's dad in the kitchen who is lovely, even though he still thinks I'm about eight years old (and who can blame him considering I don't really look that much older), and then along came Eoin.

"Sorry," he said to Donna's dad, "I'm just going to steal her away for a second."

And he grinned in this way that made me feel like I knew him so very well already, and that I could trust him, even though up until that moment he'd just been Eoin who was in some of my classes and had mostly been indistinguishable from his friends, the kind who sat at the back and messed a bit but also got involved in a lot of the Transition Year activities and did decent stuff like raising money for orphans in war-torn countries and that kind of thing. (I didn't make the connection between the fundraising and everything at the time, but at a subconscious level it probably helped. Mostly though it was the smile.)

"Thanks for rescuing me," I managed when we were out of earshot, because it seemed like the thing to say. You're not supposed to like chatting to your friends' parents, especially at parties.

He shrugged, smiled again. "You over here a lot?"

"Not, um, not – it's – I'm –" That was about the level of coherence I was managing. I paused and started again. "I've known Donna for ages, her parents seem to like me, so . . ."

He nodded and didn't roll his eyes at my inability to speak actual English, which he would have been well within his rights to do. Instead he leaned towards me and said, "I think parents always like the friends better. The friends always seem much more responsible . . ."

"And mature and sensible."

"Sensible, yeah, that's it exactly," he said, as though I had put my finger on something deep and true. "Are yours like that?"

Suddenly we were having a conversation. We stood outside the kitchen and talked and occasionally one of his friends would come over and we'd all talk and I'd wonder if I should leave now and let them talk but then he'd say something to me and make sure I was a part of the discussion and it is so strange to think of it now, as though it's a scene from someone else's life.

He kissed me at the end of the night as though it was something out of a film. Never before and never again have I felt like that, as though I was the heroine on the screen instead of the girl sitting alone watching wistfully, rewinding the good bits and sighing over them.

Sixty-eight days later I felt like the supporting character who throws herself at the hero even though the audience knows she's already lost him, crying and sobbing and begging and asking why and getting all the clichés in return. That was the start of May. Soon it'll be longer since we've been apart than we were together. Soon it'll be past the point where it is still okay to be upset about it, or to be thinking about him. Soon it will no longer be acceptable to feel as though that was just, maybe not yesterday, maybe not the day before that, but a few days ago. That it is recent and fresh.

It's not just him. It's how he made me feel, like the transformation had already taken place, like I was already captivating and gorgeous at least some of the time when we were together. But then it is him. The smile and the sort of innocent way his hair looked when he didn't gel it up and the way he'd look at me and listen to what I said and ask me questions as though the answers were really worth hearing.

12

Chloe

The first boyfriend I ever had was Raymond. It lasted most of the summer too, even though I knew it wasn't going to work out from a very early stage. We got together on the last day of sixth class and it was an excuse to be out of the house while Patrick cried all the time. I can see this now, looking back on it. I think it also had something to do with finishing primary school, this quiet little safe place where we all knew each other, and going off into a much bigger secondary school in the autumn, where I would know very few people. Neil didn't count. We weren't speaking at that point.

I suppose I was lonely. I was lonely and I was twelve years old and it was the summer after everything changed. The summer I was eleven is not one I care to remember in any great detail.

The first boy I ever had who was a friend was Neil. Maybe the first and only boy who has ever been my friend for a significant period of time before making the decision that I was not friend material but the kind of girl to be either loved or hated with no middle ground whatsoever. Eventually I became that for him too but until then we had the kind of real friendship that I don't think I've had since. But that's primary school for you, I suppose. It is impossible to keep secrets, because everyone knows everyone else and because everyone talks so openly and honestly. Everyone is too young to know otherwise.

So everyone knows what your parents work as, or what kind of family set-up you have, or what your hobbies are. You learn the words for it all in Irish. It strikes me now as an unnecessarily invasive way of teaching, getting kids to talk about their families and personal lives like that, when they are too young to realise that the world will not end if they don't do exactly what the teacher says.

What does your dad do, Chloe?

It was a small class. I was the only one who didn't have the traditional two-parent family, and when the teachers found this out they would assume that my parents were divorced. Which of course they weren't. For that one rather needs to be married to begin with.

Neil's mother was, at that point – I don't know if she still is – a stay-at-home mother, minding him and his little brother and sisters – he's the oldest of four – and I used to be so jealous of that. She was just always *there*. I had Nan and Pop-Pop of course, then, still. But it wasn't the same as having Mam there might have been.

I am far too old to be imagining what it would be like to have the kind of mother who was always there and who I could have talked to. I know that. I was lucky when I was growing up, to have had people in the family to take care of me. I am lucky now, that Martin is around, that he cares, that he comes to parent-teacher meetings and asks me how school is going and at least tries to be a good father-figure for me. I am lucky and I will not complain, not like the Boy.

Who is not the first boyfriend I've ever had and certainly won't be the last. Maybe my problem is that I have too much perspective; right from the beginning I can see that something isn't going to last, because, let's face it, what does?

13

Lynn

The first boy I ever liked was called Robert and we were in the same class, after school, for recorder. I was eight. He was nine. I asked him if he thought I was pretty, because I was eight and it was important to me to be 'pretty', and he made a face at me.

Boys generally don't find me attractive. But they have liked me, from time to time. It's flattering when they do. You'd think that occasionally one of the ones you like might like you back and at the same time, but it never seems to happen. So being liked is flattering if maybe more trouble than it's worth.

The first serious, proper, doodling-initials-in-hearts crush I ever had on a boy was on Alice's brother Jack. Three years older this time. I was fourteen. He was seventeen. I'd just finished second year, he had just finished his Leaving Cert. The fact that he thought Transition Year at our school wasn't worth doing may, in retrospect, have contributed to my skipping of it. The crush lasted longer than that summer but it's that summer I remember, because in between orchestra stuff and the Gaeltacht, I went on holidays with Alice and her family, and Jack came along for the first week of a fortnight in Portugal before heading off to Greece to do the standard mad sixth-year holiday thing. I'd watch him lying out by the pool and daydream about having late-night conversations with him out on the balcony of the apartment, where in the gentle night air he would confess all his secrets and then kiss me.

It's the oldest story in the book: girl wants boy she can't ever have.

For a while this year I wondered if liking Neil was just a way of revisiting that attraction towards Jack, or if having a crush on Jack was somehow paving the way for liking Neil. Now it feels ridiculous to even compare the two. Even so. Now that I have time to think about it, now that Neil is off speaking French with his new roommates who are apparently great fun according to his latest texts, it seems almost embarrassing. This pattern of falling for boys who will never ever ever be interested unless I suddenly turn into one of them. It is so, so stupid.

Jack was the first. But Neil is the one I wish would turn around and have a change of heart and decide that actually there might be one girl in the world worth taking a chance on, and seeing if just maybe it might work out.

Sometimes I wonder if Neil might turn out to be the first boy that I have ever loved. I dream that he might be the first one to love me. And that this summer might be the kind of summer where instead of getting a certificate of completion or accomplishment from somewhere, I get a boyfriend, instead.

Most of the time I recognise this delusional thinking for what it is, though: insanity, pure and simple.

14

Alice

I wake up on Saturday not feeling seventeen but that's how it always is with birthdays, it takes time to get used to the new age you've been counting down to for weeks or months. I lie in bed for hours, not so much enjoying the fact that I'm now seventeen but relishing the knowledge that I can lie here and don't have to go to work and smile at people and chase them around the shop hoping they'll buy something.

The door of my bedroom swings open.

"Right, I'm off," Jack announces, striding in and sitting down at the end of my bed.

"Knocking, there's this thing called knocking," I say.

He dismisses the idea of his little sister having any kind of privacy with an eye roll, and moves on. "I'm heading over to Ciarán's gaff, so here, take, little one." He hands over a card and pats me on the head. "Sure I remember when you were only a babby," he says, doing a passable imitation of our Auntie Maeve.

I sit up in bed. The card is one of those Purple Ronnie ones and there's a little packet inside. I open it up and it's a necklace, a delicate silver thing with a butterfly charm hanging on it. "Aw, Jack, it's gorgeous, thanks."

He shrugs.

"So who's this Ciarán?" I ask. "A friend, or a *friend*?"

There is more eye-rolling. "Friend," he says, and then gives me some bit of gossip, at least, maybe because it's my birthday. "For now," he adds.

I smile. "Have fun." I wonder if he will drag Ciarán back here with him this evening for the barbecue, another guest to make it an actual event.

I have the necklace on by the time I go downstairs. "Did you see this, isn't it gorgeous?" I ask Dad, who inspects it before proclaiming it to be very nice, very nice.

I feel self-conscious even when opening the presents from Mum and Dad, with only the three of us in the kitchen, the pair of them eating lunch while

I have breakfast. My work-smile is on, and I am a happy seventeen-year-old delighted with what her parents have given her, and enthusing over the books and CDs and jewellery, all thoughtfully chosen, and trying not to cry because it's always such a let-down. What I really want for my birthday is the magical transformation, a bottle of poise, a vial of beauty. I want a fairy godmother to sweep down from the skies and tap me with her wand. (It's not going to happen. That much I know. I am not completely delusional. But that it can't happen is always a disappointment. Knowing you can't have something doesn't stop you from wanting it, desperately.)

"Thank you so much," I say, and that too is awkward. Thanking your parents. I know that I should thank them more, not just when they give me birthday presents. Thank you for having me, and loving me, and taking care of me. But it's impossible to say those things, and embarrassing.

I offer to help them set up the barbecue but they've got it under control, which I am secretly relieved about. I go stare into the mirror instead. Too many spots on too pale a face. I don't look seventeen.

When I was eleven or twelve or maybe even younger, I wrote a letter to myself to be opened on my sixteenth birthday. I think I got the idea from some television programme I'd been watching, probably the same kind of programme in which all the heroine needs to do to look instantly beautiful is take her hair out of its ponytail. I assumed by the time I was sixteen I would have a boyfriend, maybe even have had lots of boyfriends. And I would have plenty of friends, and go out to parties all the time. I can't remember what else I wrote. I have no idea where the letter is. Either I put it in such a safe place that I'll never be able to find it, or – I think this is more likely – I got impatient and ripped it open six months after writing it to see if any of it had come true yet.

Today I want to read that letter, and tell my younger self that sixteen was too young for such expectations. Eighteen or maybe twenty or twenty-five: those would have been better ages.

I close my eyes and imagine being the kind of person who would have all those girls from work arriving this evening, with their perfectly painted nails and glossy hair and easy conversation. When I am twenty, maybe.

My phone rings and I panic, wondering who it is. Hoping that it is Eoin, really, and that he's remembered my birthday, and is calling to wish me a happy one, and to say that he misses me, and that I'm beautiful. Instead it's Lynn's number flashing up on the screen.

"Alice, hey. Happy birthday. What time is it tonight?"

"Um, seven," I say, "but if you want to come over earlier or anything, it's, you know, fine. Or if you're doing something beforehand . . ."

"See you at seven." And she hangs up. It's not rude, it's efficient. She is outside my front door at exactly seven that evening, the first one to arrive. Jack isn't even home yet.

If it were me I'd be panicking about being the first one there, feeling horribly awkward, but Lynn leaps into sighing in a deliberately over-the-top fashion about how young people these days just don't do time, and how it wasn't like this in her day.

"You're younger than me," I remind her, a fact which always surprises me.

"I am wise, though," she responds, and goes outside to inspect the barbecue.

Mum and Dad are doing burgers; the first batch is for us.

I look up at the sky, a pale blue dangerously close to grey. Please don't rain, please don't rain.

My phone beeps and I've something else to think mantras about. Please don't be someone saying they can't make it, please please please!

Chloe. She's really sorry she can't make it. That's it. No excuse, no reason. Chloe doesn't do excuses, of course. Because she's Chloe.

But also because I am the sort of person you can

let down and know that everything will still be okay. Docile little Alice. That is who I am.

No one ever changes, really. It's just a fantasy we like to believe in sometimes.

15

Chloe

When the phone rings it is not particularly a surprise. Nan has been taken into hospital, which we all know and no one says means that it's almost time. It's almost over.

Mam looks tight and tense and she lets Martin hold her and put his arms around her. I don't touch her. I can't remember the last time I touched her. We've never been a cuddly mother-and-daughter team.

"I'll mind Patrick," I volunteer before either of them ask, and Martin puts one hand on my shoulder and squeezes, proud of me for doing this.

For a moment after they drive away I consider taking him with me to Alice's barbecue. The event I didn't want to go to in the first place – and for a second I wonder if this is it, the universe punishing me for that, for everything.

It isn't. I don't kid myself. The universe does not punish people like that. If it did the world would be a fairer place.

I can't take my little brother to a party and talk to people as though everything is okay and not tell them what's happening, and I can almost see Alice's sympathetic face, and her well-intentioned platitudes, but also her confusion at all of this family stuff being dragged into our friendship.

It has no place there. I sit Patrick on my lap, wanting some warmth, human connection, whatever people need at a time when people are dying, but he's four. He runs off and settles himself down on the floor, in front of the television.

He looks so tiny. I am glad he's here, at home, not knowing what's going on. I am glad I'm here.

Really she's been dying for years. Since Pop-Pop 'passed on', 'went to a better place', whatever euphemism you want to use, five years ago. That summer I was eleven, the summer of everything.

I don't want to think about it. I can't stop thinking about it. Same situation, only different.

I want to talk to someone, but there is no one to talk to. I listen. I don't talk. How do I explain the full story of my grandmother who was not just the grandmother who was there to give me presents at Christmas but who was there all the time because my mother wasn't?

I pick up the phone, and need to check the phone book for the home number. I don't have a mobile number for him, and it's been too long since I rang the house. Years.

I know it's stupid even as the number is ringing. People whose phone numbers you need to look up are not the kind of people to call when you need someone.

"Hello?" It's the sister. Marie? Maria? Mary Ann?

"Hi, is Neil there?"

"Nah, he's still at French college," she says. "You can try him on his mobile, I think he's allowed use it at weekends."

"Oh, okay," I say, and she has hung up the phone before I can thank her for her help or lack thereof.

I didn't even know he was away somewhere. I just assumed. Which is what I do, I suppose. Assume, and take, and do what I want. Selfish bitch. Whore. Whatever you want to call it.

I saved a copy of Steve's rant. Not the pictures, just the text, copy-and-pasted into an email to myself from the cached page Google had stored even after it had been deleted. I am still not entirely sure why. Maybe it is good to save some things, things that people have put effort into, or maybe it is pure selfishness: this is something all about me. Even if it's hateful.

I read it over and over, hoping that it will make the tears start, but all I feel is nothingness.

16

Lynn

Sometimes I wish I had Alice's parents. Her dad's response to hearing I gave up orchestra is not "Are you sure you won't regret this?" or "Have you visualized how you'll feel about this in a year's time?" but, "Concentrating on exams, I suppose?"

I nod. Not the truth, exactly, but it's refreshing to deal with adults who see school as enough for anyone to cope with. "Yeah, next year's going to be tough," I add.

"Make sure you get a good break this summer, then," he says.

"I love your parents," I tell Jack later, who just rolls his eyes.

He hovers around when the food is being served

and then vanishes again; Alice hugs him just before he disappears instead of lecturing him on manners.

"Where's Chloe?" Donna asks. There are four of us sitting around on the fortunately still-dry grass in Alice's back garden, finishing off what's left of the burgers and salad and snacks. Alice's mum is making tea and coffee for us inside. The matter of where Chloe is, at this hour of the evening, is a good question.

Alice shrugs and puts on this voice she uses to pretend everything is all right when it isn't. "She couldn't make it."

"Oh, come on," I say. Maybe a little more annoyed about this than I should be because of Jack, who I used to adore and now see without rose-tinted glasses, or because Neil hasn't texted me in a few days, but still validly annoyed about this. This thing that Chloe does and Alice lets her do. "She had a boy thing."

"What?" Jodie says. "Aw, no way!"

I don't know Jodie that well but she, like Alice, seems to think that the world is full of nice people and any deviation from this is a surprise rather than something to be expected.

"Did she actually say that?" Donna says incredulously. Donna who has abandoned more than one of Alice's get-togethers because she's been doing something with her boyfriend, might I just add.

"No, she didn't, she just said she couldn't make it," Alice says, looking flustered. "So it's not – she – we don't know, all right? Let's not make assumptions, I mean, she's . . ."

I sigh. "It's a boy thing. It's always a boy thing." Why is there doubt in anyone's mind here?

"It could be something else," Alice half-whispers.

"Yeah, if she didn't *say* –" Jodie chimes in.

"What else could it be?" I cross my arms and look at them being so painfully naïve. "She's always doing this. Chloe's first priority is always her boyfriend."

"Who's she going out with now?" Jodie wants to know.

"Gordon – is she still going out with him?" Donna asks. "No, hold on, she's not, he was moping about her last week. John's thing," she elaborates when we look at her. "Gordon got through twenty cans that night, it was kinda scary."

"Chloe does that to guys," Alice says, almost wistfully.

"Yeah, like that's something to be proud of," I say. "She's just horrible to them, that's all."

"Ah, no, I don't think –"

"She *is*, that's all it is. She's a bitch."

Alice looks at me and then shrugs. I almost want to shake her. I want to say, you stupid girl, can't you see that she doesn't deserve to be your friend, that

80

she doesn't deserve you being nice to her? She's not here and she doesn't have an excuse and she does this all the time, abandons you for no good reason and it's always to do with a boy, because she's Chloe fucking Cullinane and everyone knows that's what she does, messes boys up and ignores her friends to do so when it suits her, and what the fuck, Alice, what's so special about her?

I breathe in and out. Deep breathing, the way Mum does it. I am calm. I am rising above it. I am not going to take any anger out on Alice for being foolish about this when really Chloe is the one who is in the wrong. I am not going to make a scene. I am not going to ruin this night. I am better than that.

"Anyway," I say, brightly, "enough about her, she's not even here. How is John doing, anyway?" I turn to Donna, who is happy to update us all.

When we all start leaving, Alice tugs at my elbow and says, "Hey, are you all right?"

"Yeah. Yeah," I say.

"You sure?" She has her concerned face on.

"I'm sure," I laugh, and wish her a final 'happy birthday' before I leave.

It only occurs to me on the way home, walking in the not-yet-darkness of summer nights, that I'm lying.

I pull my phone out of my pocket and start a text

message. *Missing you, what's up, how's life in the wilderness?* Something along those lines. I try five or six variations before giving up and deleting the whole thing without sending it. Maybe he's out of credit, or lost his phone charger, or had his phone confiscated, or maybe, just maybe, he's having too much fun to want to be bothered by me.

I miss him. I have no right to miss him this much, no claim on him, but I miss him. Insane, ridiculous, ludicrous. I want him here beside me right now, holding my hand, making me laugh, telling me I'm beautiful. The one girl who could make him reconsider what he's always believed to be true. I want to be that girl.

I miss him.

17

Chloe

Patrick falls asleep on the floor somewhere around ten thirty and I have to carry him up to bed. Adorable as he is, he weighs a ton, but once he's all tucked in I look at him fondly. Children are so cute when they're sleeping and not running around the place like lunatics or throwing temper tantrums. In September he'll be off to 'big school', even though in my head he's far too young and tiny to be going around in that grey school uniform with a schoolbag on his back, to be quizzed about his family even though his answers will be a lot easier than mine.

The time slips by while I watch him sleep, on his side, his dark hair more like mine and Mam's than Martin's, but maybe that's only because Martin is going grey already. Sometimes I imagine what it'll be like, having kids of my own, wondering if they'd look like me. Most of the time I realise I shouldn't have kids. How irresponsible would that be, to bring a baby into the world and then, inevitably, stop loving it?

It would have to happen, sooner or later. I think I stopped loving Nan the very day Pop-Pop died. It happens when you see people clearly, you see that they're going to leave, and she was just so old and frail and white, and suddenly I could see that, and that it was only a matter of time before she died too. It was just being realistic, really, and not living in this state of denial that everyone else seems to wander around happily in. Nothing lasts forever. We didn't even know about her kidneys at that point, but I could still see it – she was old. It was dangerous.

There's a key turning in the front door and I freeze. This is it. The moment they tell me. I step out of Patrick's room, close the door gently, tip-toe downstairs.

Mam looks older too, since she left earlier. She's thirty-four, almost guaranteed to be the youngest at any gathering of parents who have kids my age, but she looks like – like Nan, actually. Like Nan in her late fifties, when I was not much older than Patrick,

running after me and minding me and always being there to give me a hug whenever I'd hurt myself or was upset over something that had happened at school or something.

Martin has his arm around her. "Is Patrick asleep?" he asks me.

I nod wordlessly. It is such a strange, normal thing to ask.

"She's stable," he adds, "for now, so we're going to go back in to see her tomorrow."

"Oh," I say. "Okay."

Mam is saying nothing. Nothing at all.

I should be relieved but all I can think is that this means it's just going to last longer. Not that it's the end of this cloud hanging over us. The cloud never goes away. Anyone who thinks that way is an idiot.

"I guess I'm off to bed, then," I say, waiting for a hug, or something, anything.

"Goodnight," she says distantly, and I return up the stairs, lock myself into my bedroom, and wait for the morning.

18

Alice

The week after my birthday, one of the girls at work is out sick or on holidays or something – I don't know, not being a part of the exclusive conversations – which means that I get an extra day of work (tiring, but at least I'll have a bit more money, not that I'm spending that much – just the usual on make-up and clothes – but it's a comfort not to have to go pestering Mum and Dad for extra money). I also spend more time behind the cash register, which is a genuine treat in comparison to customer-stalking.

I am not quite sure what it is. Maybe it's the fact that here I am surrounded by equipment that stands between me and the customer, things I can check and key information into instead of having to rely on just myself out there in the dangerous forests of necklace racks and scarf collections. Or that customers have made their decisions by the time they arrive here and don't need to ask anything other than whether they can pay by credit card or not.

It terrified me at first, the tangle of technology. The first time I had to deal with a credit card I was positive I was going to mess it up in some way, overcharge or undercharge or crash the entire system. I could imagine it all so clearly: the customer being patient at first, nice, kind, so that when I kept messing it up it would be all the more unforgivable, until eventually she'd start screaming at me, demanding to know how I'd been hired and telling me that I had to be the stupidest person in the universe not to be able to do this properly. How hard is it to work in a shop, anyway? That is what a lot of people think, I have learned.

And then I didn't mess it up. It was smooth and quick and efficient and it was done. I felt like someone who was not me. My mother, maybe, or Lynn. Behind the cash register there are no opinions about what goes with what, only right answers: the amount that the customer owes you, the size of bag to give them, the change counted out into their hands. There is the obligatory thanking them, but no need to smile quite so brightly once money has exchanged hands, and there is no policy on saying something like

'Come again soon!' (which I don't think I could say with a straight face – it is far too like a parody of what we do here).

The moment at which I might stumble in this one area of work that comes easily to me happens the week the girl is off sick, when Erica from my year at school comes in. Erica is someone I have always found difficult to talk to. She is always so stylish, even in her school uniform, and there is always a boy in her life that she assumes you have heard all about via the grapevine.

I watch her browsing, ring up someone else's purchase with one eye still on her, already a little shakier about it than I usually am. I am hoping she will leave without seeing me, demonstrate that blindness to the person behind the counter that I know some people have.

Don't look at that belly-button ring with such interest, no, please, don't, don't pick it up to check the price, don't continue carrying it around with you as you wander.

I hope that Kelly, who is on customer-stalking duty today, will scare her away as she approaches, but I can see that Kelly and Erica are of the same breed. Tanned and blonde-highlighted and alarmingly similarly dressed for two people who, as far as I know, are not acquainted with one another. In fact, I think that's the same top they're wearing, only Kelly's is black (we have no uniform here, only a dress code of 'smart casual' with a side order of 'as many of the shop's accessories as you can throw on without looking ridiculous') and Erica's is olive-green.

She's heading over here. I stop breathing for a moment: do I say hi first or wait for her to recognise me? I want to duck underneath the counter and let Kelly handle the entire thing.

Erica tosses the belly-button ring and a pair of earrings onto the counter. I pick them up soundlessly, scan in the tags, concentrate entirely on that. I focus on looking focussed. I can get through this, without speaking to her, without having to confess that my summer has yet to feature any interesting trips abroad or scandalous adventures with young men or debauched drunken nights out.

"That's eleven ninety-eight when you're ready," I say, still looking at the cash register. I sneak a glance at her as she opens her wallet. She looks up.

"Oh, hi," she says. "Wow, I didn't recognise you, in your work clothes." She smiles.

I smile back. "Yeah, I'm working here." And immediately it hits me what a stupid thing that is to say.

"Any chance of a discount?" she asks, and I freeze up for a second or two.

"Um. It's already gone through, sorry," is what I finally say. And then I wonder if I should cancel it, use my staff discount, get her twenty-five percent off. We're not supposed to use our discount for buying other people stuff, but all the other girls do. With the insane mark-up on everything we sell, the profit margin is barely affected. It is the sort of nice thing – not even nice, expected thing – to do for friends who are buying something, to let them use your discount.

"Aw, boo," she says, making a face. "Oh, hey, are you doing okay?" Her tone is sympathetic. She must mean about Eoin. I am touched, and now I feel even worse about not thinking to put the discount through for her. Some people can see that it takes a long time to get over someone.

"Yeah," I say. Sort of. Maybe. I am getting better at not missing him every time there is a romantic scene in a movie and I mentally revise it with us as the leads.

"I think it's not on, personally," she says, leaning closer. "I mean, did he even ask you if it was okay?"

Do boys usually? "No, of course not," I say, and suddenly I want to cry. I am at work, I remind myself, I must be professional and smiley.

"What an asshole," she sighs. "Well, not just him, I guess, I mean she's not exactly . . ."

"Alice," my supervisor interrupts, and it takes me a moment to realise what's going on.

Erica mouths 'Sorry' at me and quickly departs as I get a reminder about not standing chatting to friends, especially when there are customers waiting to be dealt with. There's no one waiting to pay for anything, but it is probably best not to point this out.

Anyway I don't think I can say anything without tears slipping down my cheeks. I can't cry can't cry can't cry. I'm at work. I just nod and bite down fiercely on the insides of my cheeks and last maybe three agonising minutes before I excuse myself for a bathroom break. Even then I have to restrain myself, because I don't want to ruin my make-up, I have to look presentable.

Of course Erica wasn't talking about Eoin breaking up with me. That is ancient history. I am supposed to be over all of that by now, unless there is something new happening. There is a she and there is a something that he maybe should have asked me about before doing and oh God there's a she, there's someone else, he already has a new girlfriend.

I wonder if he looks into her eyes before he kisses her and tells her that she's beautiful. I wonder how beautiful she is, and if he mentally compares us, thinks that she is more attractive than me. (Oh of course he does. How could he not? It was a miracle in the first place that he ever liked me, ever even considered me.)

I wonder if they talk about me. He asked me about ex-boyfriends, early on, and I was always vague, never really admitting that he was my first real boyfriend. I thought he believed me but suddenly it occurs to me that maybe he was just humouring me. Maybe he'll tell this new girlfriend all about me, poor little Alice that he very briefly went out with because he felt sorry for her. That's the most horrific thing of all to imagine, the two of them cuddling up together and laughing at me, and this girl I don't even know suddenly having all this information about me. She will know how I kiss, and what movies make me cry at the end, and everything, everything that Eoin knows she will know because of course they will have no secrets from one another. She will be exciting and interesting enough to be honest with him about all the boys she's gone out with and all the wonderful adventures she's had in her lifetime.

Work finally finishes about a millennium after Erica's purchase, and it's raining heavily by the time my bus arrives. This seems oddly fitting and cinematic. I imagine Eoin and his new girlfriend kissing in the rain, oblivious to everything around them, and then am all too aware of myself standing alone, soaked to the bone.

On the long-overdue bus journey home, two things occur to me in sharp succession. The first is that maybe they don't talk about me at all, maybe this girl knows nothing about me, not even my name, not even the fact that I exist, and strangely enough this is a more distressing thought than the prospect of the two of them lying intertwined and mocking me.

The second is that Eoin and I have gone to the same school for four years, and that most of the people he knows are people that I know too, even if 'knowing' means 'knowing of' rather than 'knowing well enough to count as friends'. This new girlfriend of his may be a stranger, someone he's met over the summer while doing whatever it is that he's doing. Or it might be someone that I know. Not someone like Jodie or Donna, not someone I know well, but there are plenty of beautiful girls in school he might be attracted to. Or who he might have been attracted to even when we were together. (I can't think like that. I can't.)

(Except I can't help thinking like that.)

19

Lynn

"I can't believe it's July," Simon is saying, and I think but don't say that I can't believe it's *only* July.

The days are dragging by while my parents are out at work and I lounge around at home doing a horrible amount of nothing. It's depressing how the day can slide by without getting anything real done, just watching rubbish on the TV or reading rubbish online. My Bebo profile has been edited and revised so often it's absurd, and I have now been updated on how everyone I've ever known in my life is doing, including a shocking number of people I don't really care about. I am bored and wasting time, and in two days Neil is going to be home and even that seems like too far into the future to stand.

This is the kind of summer I've always half-dreamed of having: the kind with no pressure, no need to get up early in the morning to go to a class or do some activity, no real need to schedule in some time with the violin every day to be ready for orchestra rehearsals and performances. I no longer need to worry about whether my neck looks like it's been gnawed at by an overenthusiastic boyfriend when I put the violin down, or whether my wrist or shoulder is going to start acting up. I can lie around and do nothing if I want.

What do people do during the summer?

"Yeah, me neither," Kath says, stretching out on the floor. "Lynn, what have you been up to?" Shades of Jennifer-Next-Door here, I feel.

"Oh, you know, not much," I say. And then I ask, not so much because I care but to fill the gap, "What about you, what's been going on?"

Kath, who has just finished her first year at university, begins to tell me about her imminent trip off to some needy country where she will be doing good and saving the universe or something. I'm sure it's all very noble but my mind keeps slipping away. I wonder if anyone else I know will be making an appearance soon.

Every summer Simon has a party like this: a gathering of people he knows from places other than school, as most of his school friends tend to be away at this point. A reunion for everyone he's done drama classes with or debating with or been to Irish college with. His house is spacious and luxurious and his parents actually hire a cleaner, which always strikes me as a bit of an indulgence. Despite their chaotic schedules my parents and I somehow manage to keep the house relatively tidy without needing to underpay someone else to do it for us. Listening to Kath go on about her do-gooding, I wonder if her family has cleaners as well, probably overworked and underpaid, and whether she feels this is ethically compatible with her noble volunteer work.

I am self-aware enough to see that I am awkward here, that Kath is not the person I would like to be talking to. But Simon is talking to a couple of his friends that I don't know, and Kath, his girlfriend of forever and a day, is the person I am expected to talk to in these early hours of the party.

I should stop arriving on time. No one else seems to bother.

I ignore the lecture in my head from Mum about respecting one's body and accept a drink from Kath when she offers. I follow her into the kitchen as she fetches it. She's so comfortable playing the hostess, as though this is her house too.

I imagine being that comfortable in Neil's house.

Not just familiar with some of the rooms but that at ease there, as a place and not just because he's there.

I check my phone in eternal optimism or idiocy, whichever way you want to look at it. No word from him.

More people arrive, some of whom I recognise. Some of them, like Simon, have just done the Leaving Cert this year, so I ask them questions about how it went and what they're hoping to do now and let them talk.

Most people, I am realising, are not that interesting and depend an awful lot on clichés. No. I knew this already. I just have never felt it quite as acutely as now.

I move to the stairs, a few drinks later, and sit with Kath and her friend Belinda. Or maybe not her friend, maybe someone who was first Simon's friend.

I start talking and in horror I feel the tears slipping down my cheeks. Belinda makes soothing noises at me.

It comes back to me in bits and pieces the next morning, lying in bed because sitting up makes my head spin and does nothing for the churning in my stomach. I think of the Baby Book my parents used to keep, and imagine a page at the end entitled *'Lynn's First Hangover'*.

Apologising for not having anything interesting

to say because my summer hasn't been interesting in the slightest. Apologising for saying that. Orchestra and having to leave and people being mean to me. How childish that must sound. I am never drinking again. This is far too embarrassing.

Neil. Neil and love. Did I say love? Did I tell them about telling that girl in the shop he was my boyfriend?

I don't do this. I have more sense than this. I am not that girl at the party weeping in the presence of almost-strangers about issues that are far too personal to discuss at any kind of social event.

And suddenly I am so, so angry at him, for doing this to me. For not being here and for turning me into this pitiful creature.

I know it's not logical, but when you can't keep your breakfast down it's difficult to embrace logical thinking. Irrationality is definitely one's friend at times like that.

20

Chloe

I'm a horrible person. She's taking too long to die and I resent it. I just wish she'd get it over with. I am a bitch. I know this much. But sitting by her hospital bed watching her fade away is horrible. It is beyond words.

Every day when we leave we switch our phones back on and mine chimes with new text messages, all from the Boy. He wants to know if I am okay. I am waiting for the moment when he will get angry and then give up on me. It'll happen eventually. I can see it so clearly. Boys are so incredibly predictable and the only thing that surprises me is that he hasn't given up yet. It has been – no, it hasn't really been that long since we've been aware of this cloud over all of us – it just feels like an eternity.

Mam falls asleep on the sofa one night and I watch from the doorway as Martin puts a blanket over her the way they do in the films, and kisses her on the forehead. Tenderly. Like he still really loves her after all these years. He hasn't got tired of her. It's not just about Patrick, it's about her.

I try to speak and my voice won't work. I leave the room, scrawl a note to let them know I'm going out, and close the front door quietly behind me. It's still not dark out yet. There are even a few kids still playing on the road, which Nan would have never let me do, not at this hour of the night.

I walk to the Boy's house. His sister, who is irritatingly cheerful and bubbly, answers the door. "Oh, hi," she says, less enthusiastic than usual. I wonder if she's decided she dislikes me. She's at that silly age that I somehow skipped, where someone is your best friend one day and worst enemy the next and it's all usually over something incredibly trivial.

Of course it may well be that she is aware of what's been going on, my avoiding of all contact, in which case I suppose she is well within her rights not to like me.

"He's upstairs," she continues, and I make my way up to his bedroom, deciding on the way not to knock.

He's lying in bed, deeply engrossed in one of

those games that is so peculiarly male, those ones where you create your own football team and then see how they get on or something silly like that. Football and its related obsessions are one of those things that boys like to talk at you about while you nod and smile and listen. They appreciate it. It doesn't matter that you don't care as long as you pretend you do. They can't tell the difference.

I stare at him for a moment. I am waiting for him to yell at me or to be angry, but he just looks back at me.

"Hi," I say, and I bite my lip. It's not a deliberate gesture but once I've done it I remember the first night he told me he thought I was gorgeous. It was back in February, just after Valentine's Day, at this party that Alice's friend Donna was having in honour either of the holiday or of her birthday, I forget which. Larry was there, having just been dumped by his girlfriend as a charming little Valentine's Day treat, in a move that one of his friends described, perhaps unsurprisingly, as a very Chloe thing to do. He was drunk by the time we arrived, which, if his friends were to apply that same kind of honesty to his behaviour, was a very Larry thing to do, and we ended up in a bedroom somewhere, me listening to his ranting about what this girl had done and later his fond reminiscing about our own relationship. We kept being interrupted by people depositing their coats in the room, or looking for the upstairs bathroom, and early on in the night in came Eoin and then almost instantly he was backing away when he saw me and Larry in there.

"It's fine," I called out. "You can leave your stuff in here."

He paused for a moment. "Is he all right?" he asked, nodding at Larry, who had his head resting in my lap at that point. My hand was somewhere in his hair, petting him like a dog in an attempt to comfort him. I owed it to him, to listen, after what I'd done to him. He kept on saying, and it felt true, that it hurt more this time around because of how things had ended between us, it was bringing it all back up to the surface again. Or maybe he was just pissed.

"Oh, yeah," I said. "He's just . . ." And I shrugged and bit my lip and didn't know where to go from there. Just heartbroken? Just the victim of another cruel girlfriend? Just in a bedroom with me so we can talk or do you see that it's ridiculous and that by the end of the night he'll at the very least have tried to kiss me and I might let him?

He made an expression as though he understood, and left something like a bag or a jacket on the floor, and then almost as an afterthought said, "You know, you're gorgeous, by the way."

I bit my lip again. I've never been entirely comfortable when people compliment me on how I look. I see how it works. Even the plainest of girls has to be called pretty when you want something from her. But later when I thought about it, it was just a straightforward honest compliment. I was in a room with Larry, and he went and chatted up Alice downstairs, and that was all it was, a genuine statement of belief with no ulterior motives.

He's looking at me now that same way, as though I'm a beautiful person, not just on the outside but inside too. And he asks, "What are you doing here?" in this uncertain tone and it occurs to me that he thinks I'm here to break up with him.

"I wanted to see you," I say, and I realise that I'm not pretending.

I get into the bed next to him, press up against him underneath the covers. Here I can forget that I am a bad person, forget everything.

Here for the first time in what seems like forever, I am reminded of what another human being feels like.

21

Lynn

I wake up with that tingle as though it's Christmas morning and I'm five years old. Santa has visited during the night to bring forth gifts and, in this house, at least one book about getting in touch with one's creative side or finding one's inner peace.

Neil's coming home this afternoon, probably already on the road at this point, and I got a text last night inviting me over this evening for dinner. Already my mind is racing into overdrive. He'll have missed me so much that when he sees me his lips will press against mine and without realising it consciously he'll be kissing me, his feelings for me transcending any black-and-white definitions of sexuality.

Stupid, stupid. I'm not the kind of girl who makes people question a sexual identity that they've taken time to think about and reflect upon. If I'd known him when I was younger – if he hadn't been sure – if we'd been friends when we were kids –

Except he had a friend when he was younger. And well. Look how that went. I don't know why it surprised me, when he told me.

It would be stupid of me to think that all of this gay stuff is just some reaction to her, because other guys seem to have extreme, disproportionate reactions to her. It would be stupid of me to think that it might just be a way of protecting himself from future hurt, by only letting himself be attracted to guys. That is stupid, I know. I know.

Wild and improbable theories are my friend when thinking about Neil, the way that I think about him.

Dinner will be at five, he said, and I spend my afternoon trying on various outfits and not finding a single one that is just right, and hating myself for it. I feel hefty.

Fat, a voice in my head says, fat is what you mean. Let's not rely on euphemisms here.

It takes me back to that horribly humiliating night at Simon's, this feeling of wanting to cry because of not being pretty. What is 'pretty', anyway? It's a word for girls with nothing much else going for them, no interests or passions or skills apart from their borderline-anorexic bland good looks and figure.

But what else do I have going for me, now that my out-of-practice fingers move over my violin as though it's an alien artefact and I've had no one to dance around with and be silly with while Neil's away and my only other real friend is working in a shop actually being useful over the summer holidays?

I look around the house for a parent to sit with and mope with, but they're both out. They are not fans of self-pity anyway, at least not in their daughter; it is perfectly acceptable for either of them to complain about their stressful day in their lives where they have jobs they claim to love.

Dad is home in time to drop me over to Neil's house, by which point I've grown tired of feeling sorry for myself and have found something to wear and accepted the fact that I am not going to turn Neil straight simply by looking good in some particularly fetching ensemble.

For once the sun is shining as though it's remembered it's midsummer, and I'm in the house for five seconds before Neil drags me out to their back garden. We sit on the swings that are a little too small for me but I don't complain.

"Tell me everything," I say, after clinging to him for a moment. "In the form of a musical, if you like."

He leans over conspiratorially. "I made a friend."

Dagger through my heart. "Oh, I see," I say, forcing myself to beam and nudge him. "Well. I still want to know everything. All the dirty bits."

"No, no, we haven't – he's just a friend. He's coming over later, actually, and – listen, will you stay around for a bit? He's a nice guy." He looks at me earnestly, seriously. I wonder what's happened to the Neil who left a few weeks ago.

"Sure," I say. "Is he gay? Do you know?"

"Nah, he's not. He's, just, yeah." He looks away, does something with his mouth that might be a scowl or an attempted smile, and then turns back to me, the old Neil again. "So, Miss Delaney, tell me, what's been going on in your exciting life?"

I deliver an almost-truth in an over-the-top tone. "Oh, you know, I've been pining for you, darling, simply waiting around for you to return into my life and brighten it all up."

He laughs but there is something in his eyes. A wariness or something, or perhaps I'm just being paranoid.

Before he went away he would have played up to this, responded with more silliness, not simply laughed and then changed the subject, telling me that we should go inside, that dinner's nearly ready.

22

Chloe

Maybe this is it, real love, a real relationship, the sort of thing that people write songs about.

He looks at me like I'm a goddess and he hasn't given up on me and he forgives me. Love and forgiveness go hand-in-hand, don't they?

If it is love, then a lot can be forgiven.

Me being here rather than at the hospital.

Me kissing him that night in April even though he was still Alice's boyfriend.

Me going out with Gordon to try to distract myself from it all.

Me, just me, generally.

23

Lynn

The way Neil's friend Adrian looks at him is the way I look at him: a mixture of awe and lust.

Adrian arrives after dinner, after I've made small talk with Neil's family and listened to his little sister Maria go on about her new favourite pop star. I dislike him instantly.

I sit in between the two of them on the couch because Neil propels me there, and ask Adrian all the tedious questions about where he goes to school and what bands he's into.

He's being pretentious about music, which I can easily identify after years of orchestra-heads and their obnoxiousness. Music that isn't entirely instrumental and/or a century or two old and/or so obscure only three people in the world have heard of it? Heaven forbid!

"I just think," he says, "that there's no good music anymore, you know? It's *so* commercialised and it's all about making money and shit."

In my head: yeah, right, because the arts have never been about making money, because every single musician in the past did it entirely for fun, because patronage never existed, and you fucking idiot, people are always saying there's no good music anymore and do you realise what a cliché you are?

Outwardly I simply shrug and nod and let Neil and Adrian talk over me. He's Neil's friend. I can't start arguing with him and explaining to him exactly why he's so stupid.

I am rising above it all.

When Adrian's phone rings and he leaves the room to get better reception, I look at Neil. He looks smitten. The pair of them do. There is a horrible feeling in my stomach.

"I'm going to go," I say.

He grabs my arm. "No, don't. Come on, I haven't seen you in ages."

Why is it that I can't resist pleas like this? I resolve to be firm. "No, I'll leave you guys alone, it's fine."

Neil does that thing with his mouth again, looks

into space. "He'll go, if you're not here. It'll be like a *date*, it'll be weird . . ."

"But he's –" I am about to say that Adrian is obviously attracted to him. And then I stop. Why help them along? "Oh, fine, I'll stay."

I try to pretend that this is not happening. That it's not really Neil on one side of me showing off for his new friend and exaggerating stories for him. That he is not having all these in-jokes with someone who isn't me.

I've never been the delusional type.

The time passes by agonisingly slowly, my summer so far in miniature. I listen to the tales of French college and wish I'd gone, wish I hadn't thrown away my summer like this. And for what? If I'm honest, for Neil. I didn't want to spend my summer running from one place to the next and never seeing him because I was scared that if I didn't see him over the holidays we'd stop being friends. We'd return to school at the end of August and be total strangers and it would all have vanished into thin air.

I could have joined a different orchestra, a smaller one maybe, but I didn't need to throw everything away. Just because there was a group who wanted me out so there'd be a place for one of their friends, a group who decided to leave me out of all their cinema expeditions and parties and make it horribly obvious that they didn't want me around. What do you do in a situation like that? We're too old for telling Mummy and Daddy that everyone's being mean to us, and you can't make people like you.

You can't make people like you. But I wanted to, didn't I? By making myself utterly available for every whim of Neil's, every last-minute invitation. I am not a last-minute sort of girl. I am a planner. I normally hate people who ask you to do things at the last minute and assume you can rearrange your schedule to suit them.

Neil begs me to sleep over so that Adrian will. I want to say no. This was not planned beforehand. And. Well. I want to scream at him.

I don't know what I'm thinking when I say yes.

The three of us settle in Neil's room. He insists I take the bed, playing at being chivalrous. "Delicate ladies need an appropriate sleeping area," he says.

I smile a little tight smile and say nothing. No dramatic swoon and pretending to be a dainty creature who really wouldn't be able to sleep on the floor.

I am so stupid.

I toss and turn for a while, trying to get comfortable in a bed and a room not my own, and then just lie there in the hope that I'll drift off to sleep. It always takes me a night or two to adjust to a new bed.

I am so incredibly stupid.

At first I think there's something wrong. One of them is having a nightmare. I am about to turn over to face where they're sleeping when I identify the sounds for what they really are. What they must be.

I don't know exactly what they're doing. I don't want to know. I squeeze my eyes shut even though I'm facing away from them anyway. I try to stay still. The longer I stay like that the more I realise I have to stay in this frozen position. Can't move. Can't breathe. Just wait for it all to be over.

24

Chloe

It happens, finally.

I don't tell the Boy.

That night I don't want to talk, or listen, so I distract him with sex instead.

In the middle of the night I crawl out of bed, lock myself in the bathroom and wait until my heart stops pounding quite so loudly and my breathing goes back to normal before I return.

"What's up?" he says sleepily, lifting his arm from the pillow so I can slide under it and in closer to him again.

"Nothing. Go back to sleep."

25

Alice

I wake up from a tangled complicated dream in which Chloe is my sister and Lynn is an aunt or a teacher or something and I'm chasing Eoin around from dream-location to dream-location as Jack shakes his head and watches while elegantly smoking. At some point Donna turns up and marries Jack, and Eoin and I kiss in that magical movie way. I am still wistful at breakfast.

There is nothing I can do about Eoin, but it does remind me that I miss Chloe and haven't seen her in far too long. Of course, she wasn't able to come to my birthday but it occurs to me that I haven't been wonderful at keeping in touch with her since then. There is no point being annoyed with her about that.

Holding grudges does no one any good, least of all the person holding them.

I switch on my computer while I still have my morning mug of coffee in hand and send Chloe a message asking her how things are going and if she's free over the next while and wants to do something. I look it over for a moment and then send it, deciding not to obsess over how I am phrasing things for Chloe. Maybe I really am seventeen, growing up, becoming calmer about these things. Maybe by the end of the summer the sensation of my heart pounding in my chest will be a distant memory, lost to childhood like baby teeth.

I can almost see it when I look in the mirror. I do look a little older, don't I, a little less of a greasy teenager and more like a sophisticated young woman? I put on my make-up and smile at my reflection.

This week I am working four days in a row, which I force myself not to think of as four days but merely one day after another. This is not the first day of four. This is just today. It will all be okay and I won't collapse from so much smiling and everything is going to be fine. I will survive the beautiful girls and their private conversations. The customers don't know that I am not one of them.

Maybe I will get to be on the cash register today.

Maybe optimism is all it takes to be one of those confident people.

Even if Eoin does have a new girlfriend there is no guarantee that it will last. Maybe, just maybe, being with her will make him realise how much he misses me. Anything is possible.

I sail through the morning, chatting away to a customer about whether the red or green scarf suits her better and end up convincing her to buy both plus a black one. I don't even feel guilty about it. She seems so pleased with her purchase. In the afternoon, my scarf enthusiasm perfected, I compliment all kinds of colours and materials on various customers and watch them trot off to the cash register to pay for their purchases.

"Alice, hey." There is a tug on my sleeve and when I turn around it's Shelley. "These earrings are beautiful, aren't they?" she says almost absently. "Listen, I have to tell you something."

"Okay," I say, and the heart-pounding is back. Is this about Eoin's new girlfriend or is it something more serious? "Is Eoin okay?" It slips out before I can stop it.

"Oh my God, he's fine," she says, laughing, and then gets serious again. "Well, I think he's a bit of an asshole."

I can sense my supervisor hovering, and I fear yet

118

another lecture on not spending the hours I'm
supposed to be working yapping to my friends.
"Hey, Shelley, is this – look, my supervisor's going
to give out to me if I'm, you know, talking to you –
is this going to take – " I stop. I don't want to send
her away or make it seem as though I'm ungrateful
for whatever bit of Eoin-related information she is
about to pass on to me. I am in fact desperately
curious. "I'm finished up in an hour, are you still
going to be in town by then?" She hesitates, and I
add, "I know, I'm sorry, I've used up my break
already and they're really strict here . . ."

"Yeah, cool, I'll meet you here in an hour," she
says.

"Thanks," I say, and resolve to buy her an ice
cream or something to make up for this.

Suddenly my fondness for scarves is fading and I
just want to know what's going on. When the end of
my shift finally arrives, Shelley is back in the shop,
eyeing up different rings even though her fingers
are already bejewelled.

"I'm not supposed to tell you this," she starts off,
"I mean, he'd kill me if he knew I was telling you
this, but, God, my boyfriend just broke up with me
and started going out with one of my friends and I
thought, like, it's horrible, and I'd want to know,
especially if everyone else does, I mean it's so

embarrassing when you don't have a clue, you know?"

All I can do is nod and murmur. This is like a bad dream.

One of my friends. She is one of my friends after all.

And then the almost-adultness of the day slips away like a cloak, and I'm a child again, naïve and oblivious.

No. I have been, up until now. In the second before Shelley tells me who it is, I know. I know exactly. I understand it all.

Part Three

Today

26

Chloe

The clock on my bedside locker says 4:13. The two dots separating the hour and the minutes flicker. I forgot this clock did that.

This is not where I want to be. I want to be sneaking back into the Boy's room after his mother has pointedly shown me to the guest bedroom, tiptoeing past his sister's door and carefully turning the doorknob noiselessly even though his mother must know that I will always end up back in his arms anyway.

I don't know what she's so concerned about, anyway. My own mother doesn't care where I spend the night, and she's the one who should be worried. Mam has never sat me down and talked to me about boys and sex, and it would embarrass Martin to discuss it; he issues vague pleas that I return home at night rather than 'stay out'. I don't stay out. I stay in.

I wonder if it was like this for Mam, with my father, if she craved his companionship like this, if she hated having to spend nights alone in a bed that was far too empty. I can't stand being here, in this house, with these grieving people.

Nan's waxy face, not-Nan now, floats behind my eyelids when I shut them. It is so cruel, making people see their dead relatives, looking at them in that box and then chanting pointless, stupid prayers.

The funeral is in six hours and – I check the clock again – forty-four minutes.

I don't want to do this. I don't want to be here.

I know I have to be here and go to it and be respectful and not run away and curl up with the Boy somewhere. I am not a small child. I don't need to be told that I can't do what I really want to do. That's life, isn't it?

I get up, head downstairs and switch on the computer. I read my messages without any intention of responding to them. I can't, just yet. There's one from Alice from yesterday, asking me what I've been up to and if I'm around and want to do something,

123

smiley face at the end of it as always. She is such a smiley-face girl.

What can I say to that? How can I find the words to explain that I have a funeral to go to and how it fits into my life when I have spent all these years studiously avoiding comparing what-it-was-like-when-we-were-kids stories?

On the second day of secondary school we were put into alphabetical order in one of our classes, and I found myself sitting next to this girl who looked as awkward and uncomfortable on the outside as I did on the inside. I had to be nice to her. I couldn't help but be nice to her.

Sometimes, and perhaps this is a product of primary school in which you know everything about everyone else and feel entitled to personal information, people ask you questions about your family and your background and all the rest when they first meet you, as though it will tell them everything they need to know about you, as though it is a shortcut to actually spending time with you and finding out what you are like.

Alice never does that. She never has. She is so careful about not being intrusive. Even when she asks about boyfriends that I've had, they're the sweetest and safest of questions: what does it feel like when he kisses you, do you love him, do you think you have a future together? It always feels like a kiss, give or take the occasional quirk like excessive saliva or a penchant for biting. It is never love or anything with a future. They are questions that are sometimes difficult to take seriously, and to answer without rolling my eyes, but they're not dangerous or overly inquisitive.

Lynn asks nosy questions, though she's really much more comfortable talking about herself. Most people are. So you have to switch things around, make sure the conversation shifts to their own experiences. Or their opinions, in Lynn's case. I know she thinks I was too mean to Steve and am too harsh to boys in general. She talks a lot about not being able to understand why girls go out with boys if they don't respect them, that it must be simply to do with having low self-esteem and needing a boy, any boy, to make them feel better about themselves. I am so glad she skipped ahead of us this year. It gets tricky not screaming at someone for talking about things they have no real experience of. I heard she has a boyfriend now, from someone in that year, but Alice hasn't said anything to me about that and I haven't seen Lynn herself in a while to ask her about that, to see if she has mellowed now that she's found someone.

If she understood love, if I understand love now,

maybe we could actually be friends, real friends, not just friends because of Alice.

For a second I imagine my summer as though it is a glossy American film with a chirpy, bubblegum-pop soundtrack. Being surrounded by real friends, getting on well with everyone, having a boyfriend who loves me, and no attention drawn to my family.

There is nothing wrong with my family, no deep dark secrets lurking underneath the surface. Just a mother who didn't mother me, but she was young and she was working and I am probably much better off having had Nan and Pop-Pop as the ones who were there for me. I was fed and clothed and had a roof over my head. I had toys and sweets and was allowed pick the videos we rented at the weekends. And then I was eleven.

Then I was eleven.

Then I was eleven and my grandfather died suddenly and everything around me was suddenly different, and Mam was pregnant and Martin was here to stay, and the morning after that funeral I woke up with a sickening ache somewhere in my abdomen and there was blood on the sheets, everywhere. That still seems so fitting, my body realising that now there was no one to take care of me, because Nan was getting old and Mam was going to have another kid to love, and it was a forceful,

painful reminder that I was a grown-
almost.

And then I went crying to Neil and it a
there, why Chloe Cullinane is a bitch. Or do
make sense looking back on it now, to see the
pattern? If you can call selfishness a pattern.

Today it is even worse than usual to be self-
indulgent and curled up in bed crying over anything
that is not Nan. Today we are burying her. Today
cannot be like any other day, and I shouldn't be
thinking about what it would be like to have the
comfort of the Boy in bed next to me, lying
unintentionally to me and telling me that everything's
okay, because he doesn't know any better.

It is 4:34. I yawn and turn over, and then over
again, as though it will make any difference.

27

Lynn

Mum is an early riser. By the time I get up she has already saluted the sun, eaten her absurdly healthy breakfast, and taught a private morning class in our front room. When I go downstairs, she has the papers spread out across the kitchen table and is sipping away at her herbal tea as she reads.

I sit down with a bowl of cereal.

"Morning," she says, sifting through the papers. "Oh, flip it, there was something I wanted to show you, where is it?"

"Mmm," I say vaguely.

She gives up. "It's gone, it's gone. What it was anyway was – you know Trish? She's running a workshop for the next couple of weeks and she's just had a place open up if you want it, she said to tell you."

Trish is one of my mum's friends. Mum describes her alternately as a dabbler in everything, an incredible woman, and a poor thing in need of settling down, depending on how much she's had to drink and whether she and Trish are having one of their arguments or not. You'd think my mother would see the hypocrisy in drinking at all when she's usually so fussy about putting 'poisons' into her body, or in having a friend she can't stand half the time, but. Well. Adults. Honestly.

"What are they doing?" I ask. I've always been torn between wanting to do one of her workshops and being glad that the timing hasn't worked out so I don't have to. She seems a little disorganised and up in the air about the whole thing, basically deciding what she's going to do on any given day at the last possible minute.

"A bit of drama, bit of yoga, some music, oh, you'd love it," Mum says.

"Maybe," I say cautiously. After being my mother for nearly seventeen years, she still hasn't quite copped on to the fact that I'd rather dance and move about than stay still and do deep breathing while my body is contorted into some weird shape.

She looks at me. "It'd be good for you to get out of the house."

"I do get out of the house."

She sighs. "This isn't like you, sweetie. How are your energy levels? Should we get you a tonic or something?"

"Only if it comes with gin," I say almost without thinking.

"Oh, you're not drinking *gin* these days, are you?" Mum sighs. "You're too young to be drinking spirits, honey – I know you've probably stopped growing, but still . . ."

"I'm too young to be drinking, full-stop," I remind her.

She rolls her eyes and waves her hands about. "Yes, yes, of course, but you know what I mean. Your father and I don't mind if you drink a little, just be *sensible* about it."

"I'm always sensible," I say, which is obviously a lie, because I was not sensible with alcohol at Simon's thing, and I was certainly not sensible with life when I agreed to stay over at Neil's house that night.

"I know you are, of course you are. Will I tell Trish to keep that space for you?"

"I don't know. Is there a schedule or anything I can look at before I make up my mind?"

Mum rifles through the papers again. Fruitless search. "Sorry, honey, I had it somewhere . . . anyway, you know what Trish is like – you just have to go with the flow."

"I can't 'go with the flow' – God, would it kill her to act like an actual adult and be properly organised about it?"

"No need to snap at me," Mum says sharply. Amazing how little it takes to shake her out of her mellowness.

I get up and leave the table. I am not in the mood for this right now. I eat the rest of the cereal in front of the television.

Committing myself to anything at the moment seems like too much effort when it is so much easier not to do it. Even though I'm bored. Even though it might be a fun and useful and worthwhile thing to do.

Sitting around moping about Neil is not worthwhile.

Today I'm meeting him for coffee before he and Adrian go see something in the IFI. He must know that it's about that night. I left before the two of them woke up the next morning, and when he texted me about today I told him that I would meet him only if Adrian wasn't arriving 'til later.

I don't want to see Adrian. I really don't. I'm not even that sure I want to see Neil.

When you're annoyed with someone, when you're angry, you tell them, you get it out in the open, you stop being friends with them if you can.

Neil and I don't have any mutual friends to appease, or situations we absolutely have to be in together; we could easily avoid one another next year if we wanted to.

I don't want to avoid him. I just want to be his friend. But his friend before all of this happened, before he went away, before Adrian came along. I don't think I can see him today and still end up being his friend.

I said I would see him later. I will not cancel. I'm not like that. I just wish for a moment I was the sort of girl who could cancel, and avoid his messages, and avoid the inevitable moment where I tell him exactly how much I hated being in that bedroom with them, and how much I hated him then.

I would be grateful to the universe if time could stop today and if it never has to happen. That would be nice.

28

Alice

How is it possible that only yesterday work seemed like such a reasonable, easy thing to get through?

I hit the snooze button on my alarm clock again, even though most of the world has probably already got up at this point. It is not an early morning for me today but it feels like one, that same sense of being not quite able to get out of bed just yet.

I contemplate calling in sick, but that would mean talking to my supervisor, and I am sure she would be able to tell that I am not genuinely ill. I am a hopeless liar, even over the phone, and being nervous about talking on the phone anyway doesn't help. There is something about not being able to see people's faces that makes the business of communicating with people over the phone even more difficult than dealing with them in real life, especially if they're someone you don't know very well or need to impress because they're the ones deciding whether you can keep your job or not.

I can't call in sick. It is not an option, as appealing as it seems. This is my job. I have to be there. Those are the rules. I can't get Mum to write me a sick note and let me off the hook.

So I get up, later than I need to, and run for my bus. For a second I worry that it will trundle off before I can make it to the stop, but the bus driver seems to have a conscience and waits until I get there.

I want to say thank you. It is incredibly rude not to, but if I say anything I will burst into tears, so I just fish out the right change for the fare and smile weakly at the driver and hope that it's enough. Please don't think I'm rude, please please please. It's just that I was worried you wouldn't stop and then I wouldn't get to work on time and then I'd lose my job and I'd be marked forever as irresponsible and not worth employing and one of my alleged best friends is going out with my ex-boyfriend and I cannot believe I didn't see it coming.

My birthday, my birthday, she couldn't come to my birthday and Lynn thought it was a boy thing and of course it was, it was an Eoin thing. And of course he's attracted to her, the way that boys always are to Chloe, because she's a fairytale princess and the beautiful perfect girl of everyone's dreams. Of course, it is all so obvious. And Erica knows, which means everyone must know, and these extra little details keep occurring to me the more I think about it. I will go back to school at the end of the summer and instead of being magically transformed I will be a pitiful creature, that girl who used to trust Chloe and who took longer than everyone else to figure out that Chloe is not the kind of person to be trusted.

Everyone else already knows this about Chloe. She has more friends than I do, in the sense that she gets invited to parties, or out clubbing, but there is no one who really likes her, and she is invited mostly, it seems, because the boys at school are all in love with her. I know all of this. I have listened to the gossip and the bitching and even though I have never quite managed to stick up for her and say that she is a good friend and a good person and doesn't deserve to be talked about behind her back, I have always known that they're just jealous of her. It always made sense to me. Of course they were jealous of Chloe, and wanted to be her. How could you *not* want to be her, to effortlessly attract the boys the way she does, to be as sure of yourself in your skin as she is?

I cannot cry on this bus. I close my eyes and think about scarves and jewellery and flip-flops and hair clips. I am going to go to work. I am going to be okay. Everything is going to be fine. I will not think about Chloe or Eoin.

I will think about positive things, like my skin not looking as disastrous as it normally does, which is fortunate as I didn't have time this morning to do my make-up properly. And Shelley coming to talk to me yesterday, which was kind of her. Think about how much worse it could have been not knowing until we all went back to school. (Think about how much easier it would have been not knowing, how much hope I would still have.)

I realise that we've arrived at my stop just in time, leaping up and chasing a happy couple down the stairs and out into the street. I elbow my way past them in their hand-holding cuddliness, their couple-ish joy, and race into work.

29

Neil

"God, Maria, shut up!"

It's way too early in the morning for this crap. All right, it's not that early, but my little sister practising her singing is not something you want to hear at any hour of the day. When she does solos and stuff at Mass or at school things she's grand, but around the house it's like she has to go over the top with it and act like she's an opera singer, complete with dramatic gestures.

"I have to practise," she says in her know-it-all way. "I can't turn up at a *christening* and sing badly, can I?"

"Maria, maybe leave it until after you've left the table, okay?" Mom intervenes. She puts down the plate of pancakes in front of us, and we start grabbing. Mom's pancakes – these I missed when I was away. Unlike the sister. Well, this one. Sophie's eleven, only just starting to get annoying. And then Oisín's eight, and already has a 'girlfriend' from his class at school, which doesn't bode well for me.

"So what are you doing today?" Mom asks. "Seeing Lynn at all?"

Mom *loves* Lynn. Half because Lynn is fabulous with parents and half because I think Mom hopes she's my girlfriend.

I stuff my mouth with pancake so I don't have to answer right away. "Yeah," I finally say. I don't add that I'm seeing Adrian later and that's the important part. Not that Lynn's not important, but she's just a friend, and it's different.

I have someone, and I can't tell Mom because she'd freak out and then wonder where she went wrong, as though she had anything to do with it. I have someone, and I didn't think I ever would. It sounds stupid, I guess. But when you're in school and people go around saying 'that's so gay' to mean that something's stupid, you don't really see yourself ever finding someone, not at this age. I figured I'd have to wait until college, which seemed like ages away, even with skipping fourth year, and be doomed to having crushes on random guys from afar because there's no way, at our school, you could ever let someone know that you liked him. You'd get the shit kicked out of you in no time.

I used to imagine that all I'd ever have would be good friendships with people, girls I mean, like Lynn, where we'd be really close and tell each other stuff and have people assume we were in a couple but not actually be because of the obvious. Honestly, it doesn't hurt to have people think you have a girlfriend. You can get away with a hell of a lot of campness when it's directed at the girl everyone thinks you're going out with. I mean, we had a lot of fun together over the last year. School was definitely more bearable. But it's not the same as having someone who you just click with, the way me and Adrian did. I wasn't sure at first whether he was gay or not. I mean, okay, I was pretty sure he was, but that could have just been wishful thinking getting in the way. And we got on really well, even though he panicked whenever the conversation veered towards anything that might be a step closer to him having to actually say whether he was or wasn't.

When the course was over and nothing had happened, I figured I'd ask him if he wanted to come over to my house that night and at least if he freaked out then, I'd never have to see him again if I didn't want to. He doesn't even go to school in Dublin, he lives out in Kildare, which means we've this running joke about his culchie background and all that, how he didn't hear about the internet 'til last year and then tried to write on the screen with chalk, that kind of thing. He got this panicked look in his eyes and I said that one of my friends was going to be staying the night and it'd be cool for us all to hang out together, and he relaxed and it was all grand.

I mean, I think Lynn's still a bit pissed off about it. She left in such a huff the next morning, but what can you do? I'm seeing her later so hopefully we can get it all sorted out. She made such a big deal about not wanting Adrian to be there. You'd think she'd be happy that I've found someone. I'd be thrilled for her.

Girls. I mean, it's not like I *chose* not to fancy them, but seriously, sometimes it feels like a good move on the part of fate or whatever, letting me escape having to put up with that kind of bullshit from the people I'm into.

30

Gemma

Supervisor-Bitch is on the warpath again. Sorry, actually, when is she ever not on the warpath? Don't chat to the customers if you're not making a sale! Don't stand around yapping to one another even if there's no one in the shop!

This is the problem with shop jobs, having to make yourself look busy because of the customers, always think about the bloody customers. Next summer I'm so getting a job in an office somewhere, where I can sit at a desk and not have to worry about customers. I almost got an office job this year but they wanted someone with more experience and I've only ever worked in shops. How are you supposed to get the experience if they won't let you work there in the first place, that's what I want to know. But at least next summer I'll have a year of college under my belt, hopefully. Fingers crossed. I swore I wasn't going to be like my sister panicking about Leaving Cert results. She went mad last year, spent the whole summer chewing on her nails and fretting about whether or not she'd passed everything and whether she was going to get into any of the courses she'd put down. I'm surprised she didn't give herself an ulcer or something. And then she got something like a hundred points more than she needed for the physics course she'd put down at the top of her list. Bloody genius.

I so wouldn't be able to hack it in physics or anything like that – my brains would start dribbling out of my ears. I've got social science down at number one or number two, I forget now which one it is. I kept changing my mind. I have loads of variations on a theme, they're all called social science or sociology or something like that, at different colleges. Some of them are more 'academic' and some of them are more 'vocational', and would you look at that, I actually did pick up something from all those sessions with my careers teacher last year, running in and out of her office all the time asking her what she thought of this course and that one. Some of them are more practical and you can go on and be a social worker or something like that. I'm trying not to think about it too much. I don't know if I'd be any good at that kind of thing but the courses look interesting and I'm good at writing essays and stuff, much better at that than prancing around a shop telling people that those earrings come with a matching necklace or whatever.

"Where the *fuck* is Alice?" Supervisor-Bitch demands of me, as though I have any idea. So tempted to remind her that she should keep her voice down, even though there's only one customer on the other side of the shop who probably hasn't heard her.

I shrug. "I don't know, sorry." *Obviously*, you mad cow. Give the poor girl a break. Alice is this lovely kid who's always in on time, let her away with being, what, five minutes late, this once.

"There you are." She's not talking to me this time.

Poor Alice has just arrived, looking completely out of breath and terrified. Kelly, one of the other girls, thinks Alice is a bit up herself, that she thinks she's better than us or whatever, but I think she's just shy. Or else she could be really focussed on her job – that's maybe why she doesn't like chatting to us during work time. It's probably her first job – she looks young enough.

Alice gets sent off to the storeroom, which is a horrible place to be for any more than an hour. It's all dark and cramped and by the end of it you're ready to go ballistic. Supervisor-Bitch comes over for one of her periodic attempts at camaraderie, needing someone to bitch with.

"Jesus, that girl shouldn't be allowed out of the house without make-up," she says.

I didn't even notice. How much difference can it even make? God, she's such a *bitch*. That's got to be on some list of really unprofessional things to say about people you work with, especially *to* other people you work with. Fingers crossed for getting a better job next summer, with semi-decent people telling me what to do. I'm not sure I can stick another summer of this. Instead of maybe becoming the kind of person who provides professional help, I'd have to start seeking it out. I'd suggest to Supervisor-Bitch that they offer free therapy along with the discount for working here, but I bet she'd eat me alive . . .

31

Chloe

"You're not wearing that," Mam says flatly.

"What's wrong with it?" It's black. It's a black top and black trousers and it's all clean, what more does she want from me?

She glares at me. "You can't wear that," she says, and walks off.

"Fine, then I won't go!" I scream after her.

She spins around on her heel and slaps me across the face. I suppose, on reflection, I deserved that.

Martin intervenes. "Chloe, come on, let's go find you something else to wear. Lydia, Patrick needs to get dressed, you should go –"

"I have to get ready myself," Mam snaps at him, even though she's already dressed.

"Okay. Okay. I'll sort him out after we find something for Chloe."

"What's wrong with what I'm wearing?" I demand the second we're in my room.

He sighs. "I think it's fine, but – look, this is a hard time for everyone, all right? Especially your mam. Just be patient with her."

"She slapped me," I say, even though I know that I shouldn't have threatened not to go to the funeral. I'm so petty. Petty childish Chloe. And I have no idea what's wrong with what I'm wearing.

"I know, I know." He runs his fingers through his hair and I wonder how much of that greyness is to do with the fact that he is married to my mother. "She's – look, we weren't going to say anything until we're sure, but –"

"She's pregnant," I say. "Well. Whoop-de-doo." Is this a compulsion of hers, the filling up of the gaps in her life with new babies? Who was I a replacement for? Oh, no, that's right – I was the awkward one, the one who made things more difficult for her. Not like Patrick. Not like this new baby-to-be.

Martin looks disappointed in me. "Don't be like that. You love Patrick, don't you?"

I sigh. "Of course I do." I manage a smile. "And of course I'm going to love this new baby. Who doesn't love kids, right? You'd have to be a total monster not to love kids, wouldn't you?"

If he detects any undertones, he doesn't comment. "Here, put on a shirt instead of that yoke, it looks a bit better." He takes out a black short-sleeved blouse from my wardrobe. I don't even know if it fits me anymore. I've had it for years.

Martin leaves me to get changed and I look at myself in the mirror. Is this more appropriate funeral attire? I can't stand wearing black. It is such a depressing colour. I look like a faded-in-the-wash version of myself.

What did I wear last time? I can't even remember. Did she get angry with me that day, too?

I'm being a brat here. Martin is right. It's difficult for all of us. And pregnancy makes people crazy anyway. I have to remember not to complain, even inside my head. I think about the Boy and the way he goes on about his family, and how I can see that they love him despite everything.

Oh, who am I kidding? Mam doesn't love me. She doesn't care where I spend the night, or how I'm feeling, or anything. She cares about herself first and foremost. She just wants Martin to take care of her, that's the only reason she's with him.

We go to the church and I sit near the back with Patrick.

"Now, if he starts making a fuss, just take him outside for a bit, it's fine," Martin says to me, squeezing my shoulder, before he goes and sits up at the front with Mam.

I could have sat up the front, near the coffin, if I wanted. I could have done a reading, but I didn't want to. Just because it's Nan's funeral doesn't mean that I've suddenly started believing in the whole business. Nan was a believer, of course. At her age I suppose you'd want to be.

Mam's brothers and sisters are up at the front too, with their respective spouses. Most of them are only starting to have kids now, even though she's not even the oldest of them all. They live abroad, in England and in France and in Australia and the States. They have exciting lives and wonderful careers. They didn't have their lives messed up by an unwanted daughter.

One of my aunts, my uncle's new wife, asked me yesterday if this was my first funeral, the first time I've been through all of this. She's new. I suppose it isn't fair to remind her that this is the second death in five years. Maybe in some families this wouldn't even be excessive. Maybe in other families there is much more loss. Maybe we are lucky.

Patrick is shifting restlessly next to me. He knows he has to be quiet, the poor thing, but he doesn't entirely understand what's going on. Part of me is hoping he starts crying or throwing a temper tantrum or something, so I can get out of here. I can empathise with the restlessness. I just want this to be over.

The priest names all the grandchildren together, including the cousins of mine I hardly know, as though we are all equal. As though they even knew her.

I hate all this religious nonsense. Patrick leans against me and starts drifting off to sleep. I wonder if that counts as being disruptive. If he starts snoring I could take him outside, out into the sunshine. Today, of all days, the sun is beaming down on all of us.

And afterwards, all the hand-shaking, the clichés. I am so sorry for your loss. I am glad that I'm not up there, receiving the fake sympathy. I am glad that when this is all over, I can return to my life and no one will feel the need to say something, as though anything they say can change anything.

I watch them, all of the siblings together. They're all at least a little bit teary-eyed, apart from Mam, who is the one who should be. She's the one who stayed here, who didn't go away, who's watched Nan fade away for the last five years. What's wrong with her, that she can't feel anything, that she can't cry, today of all days?

What's wrong with me, when my eyes are still dry and all I want to do is run away from this miserable church and never come back? I wonder if her brothers and sisters have noticed, if everyone here is looking at me and thinking, ah, Chloe, you really are your mother's daughter, aren't you? How damning, how true.

32

Eoin

She's not picking up her phone, which is fucking typical of her. I'm having the ten millionth argument with my dad about my 'attitude problem' because I got in late last night, as though two in the morning is actually so late that you need to worry instead of early by most normal people's standards, and is it too much to ask that someone who's supposed to be your girlfriend actually answers her phone every once in a while?

This is the problem with Chloe, she goes hot and cold on you. It's masochistic, putting up with her, except most of the time she's great. Amazing, even. For starters she's totally gorgeous, but it's not just that. It helps, obviously. All that 'what's inside' stuff all well and good but you need to be attracted to someone first off, before you get the chance to find out what they're like as a person.

The girl I was with before Chloe, Alice – who's actually a good friend of Chloe's and would completely overreact if she knew I was with Chloe now, so we're keeping it a bit quiet for now – is sweet but she'd freak out if you wanted to do anything more than score, like it was instantly going to lead to her getting pregnant or something. It's not like I even wanted that. Not immediately, like. Jesus. And I know that some girls do get really paranoid about that, even if you don't even have sex but just do all that other stuff, which is a bit mental but maybe I'd panic if I knew something could start growing inside me too.

I don't know if I'd have even minded so much about Alice if she hadn't at the same time been so lovey-dovey about holding hands and saying how much she liked me and all that stuff. Maybe she thought it was what I wanted to hear but it's hard to believe it from someone who pushes your hand away when you try to move it anywhere underneath any item of clothing. She'd probably have panicked if I slid a finger under her, like, sock or something stupid like that. I liked her and everything but Chloe just makes a lot more sense. Even aside from being gorgeous – and Alice is pretty and all, but not the way Chloe is. She listens and she laughs at all the right parts, and she really seems to care when you're talking to her about family shit or whatever. And she's good at taking your mind off things, which is a nice change. Even the way she kisses, Jesus. We scored one night at this party back when I was still with Alice, a bit drunk, whatever, and it was amazing.

I know she has a bit of a reputation. I'm pretty sure she doesn't deserve it. Girls, especially, are just so horrible about each other sometimes. I really don't get it, but let them at it. Ask any of the lads in school what they really think of Chloe Cullinane and they'll admit they'd totally be with her if they were given the chance. She's hot. It's that simple. You can't take Steve's whining about her too seriously. Obviously he's not going to be thrilled if someone like Chloe breaks up with him. Deal with it, get over it.

And there's obviously something going on at home that she doesn't want to talk about. Maybe her stepdad or something. There's something, you can just tell. She's not just one of those girls who decides she's fed up with you. I just wish she'd actually talk about it, instead of going through these phases of ignoring me and avoiding me.

I run through the numbers in my phone. Loads of people from school, but I don't think any of them would know where she is or what's going on with her. I go all the way through the alphabet before starting over.

Alice doesn't even know we're together. Hardly anyone knows. Shelley does, because she sticks her nose into everything, but she knows she's not supposed to say anything until me and Chloe have agreed that Alice will be okay with it, and Chloe's friend Erica from school knows because she saw us together this one time, but any time I've heard her talking about Alice it's always been bitching about her so it's not like she's going to go running off filling her in on all the latest gossip. And that's it. It'll be fine by the time we get back to school. Alice is just so sensitive. It's not worth the hassle. That battle-axe friend of hers would probably hunt you down and kill you or something.

And if there's something going on with Chloe, she'll know about it. I mean, I should know, if there is.

I call her.

33

Shelley

Best day ever. Oh my God. This completely makes up for the fact that Janice is a total slut and stole Matt away from me. Two days of not speaking to each other does not a break-up make. Honestly. I actually can't believe her. I'm still not talking to her.

But this is making up for it. Well, maybe not entirely but it's helping. Rosie got this makeover voucher thing for her birthday and she's being really generous and using it to get three basic sessions instead of one big super-intense one, so me and her and her sister Erica are getting our faces done and feeling very posh and fancy. I want to buy everything that they're using. I totally would if it wasn't for Rosie nudging me and reminding me that I can't afford it. I wish I was old enough to have a job, or that Mum and Dad would give me more pocket money. They give Eoin way more money than me, even though he's old enough to get a part-time job if he could be bothered. He couldn't, though, that's the problem, he's so lazy. All he does is play games and watch TV and do whatever it is he does with his girlfriends – I don't even want to know.

"Maybe just the foundation," I say at the end of the sales pitch, even though it's all my pocket money for the week gone. But it suits me, and these are professionals doing this, they know what the good-quality stuff is. And you don't want to be putting cheap stuff on your skin, you'll regret it when you're older.

It's really worth putting in the effort to look well. That's what life is all about, really. It's all well and good to be brilliant at school but if you don't look the part, no one will care. No one gets a chance to see what you're like on the inside if the outside isn't worth getting to know. Mum spends a fortune on creams and lotions and potions to keep her skin in good shape. I wish she'd buy stuff for me, but she keeps on saying that I'm still young and don't need to worry. I think now is the time to worry. If I don't take care of my skin now, I'll really wish I had by the time I'm her age. Even though she doesn't look her age. Dad's always telling her how beautiful she looks, how young for her age she still looks.

"I can't believe you spent that much money on foundation," Rosie hisses at me as we go off to lunch, still all done up and looking spectacular. Her mum is taking us to lunch so I don't need to worry about being broke. It's fine.

"It's worth it, if it suits you," Erica says wisely. I wish I had an older sister like her. She'd give me good advice about Janice and Matt. I went to talk to Alice yesterday and she let me rant about it, but it's not the same. And I felt kind of bad about going on about it anyway when I'd just told her about Chloe and Eoin. I seriously can't believe my brother. Everyone knows you're not supposed to go out with your ex's best friend unless they specifically say that it's okay. And Alice is cool, she's working in the best accessories shop ever and she's clever and I bet she's had loads of boys interested in her, even if she made the stupid decision of going out with my brother rather than anyone else.

"So how's your brother doing?" Erica asks me as we sit down to lunch in this really fancy place that me and Rosie would so never be going to if we had to pay for it ourselves.

I never go to anyplace where they come around and ask you what you want to order instead of having to go up to the counter, except when we have a family dinner out. And this place has super-comfortable chairs and loads of space between the tables so that the people next to you aren't bumping your table when they get up.

"Oh my God, he's, you know, whatever, his usual self," I say. And I know I'm not supposed to tell anyone about him and Chloe, but I already told Alice so it's sort of too late to keep it a secret anyway, so I add, "You know he's going out with Chloe Cullinane, right?"

"You're kidding!" Rosie says.

Chloe is practically a mythic creature at our school. There are all these stories about her, like that she broke up with that guy who killed himself and that's why he did it, or that she's a total whore and sleeps with everything that moves, or that she once had a thing with her boyfriend and his ex at the same time . . . loads of stories. I don't know how much of it is true. She's not that friendly, when she comes over to see Eoin. She's sort of cold, and I don't think she's even that pretty, really.

"No, really," I say, and look at Erica to see what she thinks. She's in their year at school.

"Really," Erica adds.

"Oh my God, how do *you* know?" I can't believe someone else knows when it's been such a big deal for me to keep it a secret and not tell anyone.

"I saw them together," she says. "It's *so* obvious. Poor Alice, though."

"Yeah, I can't believe him, she's so nice," I say.

Erica makes a face. "She's sort of weird. But like, *still*. That's what you get when you're friends with someone like Chloe. And poor Eoin. She's going to *crush* him."

Oh my God, Erica likes Eoin. I understand that look. What is wrong with the girls of that year? Is there something in the water? Why are they all after my brother? He's just some lazy slob who won't listen to Dad when he says he should get a summer job or start working harder in school or figure out what he wants to do with his life. Next thing I know Rosie will be after him.

I like talking about all this stuff, though. Even though it's completely insane that sensible girls are into Eoin. It's a nice distraction from the idea of Janice and Matt off somewhere, her tongue stuck down his throat. Really, what sort of friend *does* that, anyway?

34

Alice

In the storeroom, sorting through boxes of things, counting and cataloguing, I am much happier than outside. If only I could be in here all the time, away from all the other girls and the reminders that I don't fit, simply allowed to do my job in peace and quiet and not having to worry about what people think of me. If only there was enough work to do here to keep me busy for the rest of the summer.

Something is ringing in my pocket. My phone. I forgot to turn it off or switch it on silent the way I usually do. Most of the time I don't even need to worry about it, because it is not as though I am the kind of girl people ring up constantly.

My supervisor is going to give out to me if I'm

talking on the phone during work time. She's already annoyed because I arrived in late. I'm about to switch it off and call whoever it is later with an apology and an explanation when I see who it is calling.

I should have deleted his number from my phone, I suppose, drawn a clear and decisive line in the sand and accepted that it was over. If I had done that back when we broke up maybe things would be easier now. (Not when we broke up. When he broke up with me. I must at least try to live in the real world and not the movie version I would like to live in.)

It only takes a split second for the fantasies to start flooding in again. He's seen the error of his ways and he wants to get back together with me. He's realised that he really does care about me, and he's going to apologise for everything and then he'll turn up and kiss me and everything will be magical and wonderful. He's calling me, that's the important thing, he's calling me and he wants to talk to me and how can I not answer this call even if I am at work?

I am trembling. "Hello?" I say, struggling to sound calm and nonchalant even though it is the hardest thing in the world to do. This is Eoin, after all.

"Hey, Alice, how's it going?"

I almost melt at his voice. It's like things used to be, this familiarity between us. I miss that.

"Um – fine, it's fine," I say, tingling and anticipatory. Why are you calling me, Eoin, oh never mind, just talk to me. Just remind me of what it's like to be your girlfriend.

"Listen, can I talk to you for a second?"

"Sure." Anything. Anything at all you want.

"You don't happen to know where your friend Chloe is, do you? I need to talk to her about something."

"Uh . . ." I say. And for a moment I'm so caught up in the fact that he's asking me something, and wanting so desperately to be able to give him an answer, that what he's actually asking me doesn't sink in.

And then it does.

"What?" I say, because that's all I can think of to say.

He goes on, some story about how he needs to get in touch with her and he's worried that there might be something going on and never once does he mention the obvious, which is that out of the two of us, he's far more likely to know where she is. In his bed, probably.

Oh no no no, please don't let them actually be sleeping together! Oh but Chloe would, maybe, she doesn't seem to think it's a huge deal even though it obviously is.

162

"I just think she needs someone to talk to," he is saying, and suddenly I am back a week or so before we broke up, at a party one of his friends had, and I am feeling out of place because without Eoin by my side these people are a little bit more intimidating and it is almost like how things were before Eoin and I started going out. Chloe is here but I have no idea where she is, and it is best not to hunt her down in case she is off with some boy, and then someone tells me she is out in the garden. I push the door open and, even though I hate calling out people's names because it just feels so silly, I have had a couple of drinks because it is hard to say no to Eoin's friends, and so I call out something like, "Chloe, are you out here?"

And she emerges from around the corner, around by the side of the house, and says hi, and looks strange in a way that I can't quite classify, and for a second I think she's out here with some boy, but then Eoin follows her out and I am so glad to see him that I don't think.

"I just think she needs someone to talk to," he says to me a minute or so later, even though I have not asked any questions, and then he tells me that he's glad to be back inside with me, and I light up all over.

"Eoin," I say now, interrupting his storytelling. "Can I ask you something?"

"Of course," he says, casual as anything.

"When we were together," I say, and it is so hard to find the words for this, and to keep my voice steady, "um . . . I was just, you know, wondering, when we were together, if you ever, like, cheated on me."

He pauses. "Why would you think that?"

"Just wondering," I say.

"God, that's ancient history, anyway," he goes on like I haven't said anything.

"That's a yes, then," I say, and there is silence.

I hang up at the precise moment my supervisor storms in and says, "Alice, I'm not paying you to yap to your friends, you know."

I try to say sorry but the words won't come. I can't talk. I simply can't.

"Honestly, you come in late, looking *completely* unprofessional –"

"What?" I whisper.

She sighs in exasperation. "You have to look *presentable*, Alice, not like you just rolled out of bed."

I can't even take that in right now. I am hardly aware of what's going on.

"And talking on your phone during work time is completely unacceptable. I hope you don't think you're getting a lunch break after that, I don't care how important it was."

She goes on and on and on.

I have to get out of here. I just have to leave. I have to –

"I quit," I say, and because the only thing to do after saying that is walk off, that is exactly what I do.

35

Lynn

A shocking amount of the morning has gone by in a daze in front of the computer, except that it's stopped being shocking anymore, when Dad pokes his head around the door and asks if I made tea.

"It's in the pot," I say, and then realise that was probably an hour ago. "It's probably cold now, though."

I join him in the kitchen as we wait for the kettle to boil. Mum has gone off to teach her classes at a community centre a few miles away, and Dad is just up, having been out at work until late last night.

"What are you doing today?" he asks, picking up the newspapers Mum has already made her way through.

I shrug. "Nothing, really. Seeing Neil. The usual."

"Mum was telling me about that workshop Trish is doing."

"Yeah. I don't know if it's really my thing."

"It seems like a good opportunity. And it'd get you out of the house."

"Have you and Mum been having a chat about 'getting me out of the house'?" I look at him, my arms folded. "Do you want me 'out of the house'?"

"Don't be silly. We're only thinking of you. Are you not bored out of your mind, just 'hanging around'?"

Yes. Yes, completely and utterly, and at the same time it seems like so much effort to turn back into the Lynn who was busy. Neil has sucked the life out of me.

"No, it's fine," I say. "You know, I have exams next year, some parents think it's a good idea for their kids to actually get a break before they start studying like a lunatic. Some parents just accept their children for who they are instead of pushing them into stuff."

"No one's pushing you into anything," he says. "If you don't want to do the workshop it's fine, no one's going to make you do it. We just thought it might be something you'd enjoy."

I sigh and accept the tea when it's poured. Back to the computer to perhaps go and join a forum to discuss foolish infatuations with one's gay friends.

My phone's ringing. Alice.

"Hi," I say, "how are you doing?"

"Hey," she says, shakily, "are you – are you in town or anything?"

"Nah, I'm heading in later. Are you okay?" What a stupid question. She doesn't sound it.

"I quit my job!" she wails.

"Shhh. Calm down, okay? I'll come in and we'll go get ice cream and we'll talk about it, all right?"

"Ice cream would be good," she sniffles.

I laugh. "Okay."

Now this is something that, unlike the Neil debacle, I can actually handle.

36

Jack

So the plan is to go and meet Ciarán for lunch, on my break from showing groups of tourists around college and waiting patiently as they take photos of things and go 'ooh' and 'aah' over being in a 'real old' college. Those would be the American tourists, anyway. Maybe tourists of other nationalities and languages express similar sentiments and I just don't understand them. I don't know. They probably come from places where something more than fifty years old isn't considered an ancient relic.

It's a handy enough job, anyway, right in the centre of town and college looks pretty decent when it's sunny out, like today. It's a pity the weather isn't like this all year round. In the rain everything just looks grey, never mind the historic buildings or whatever, but everything looks grey anyway when you study science and are trying constantly not to be bitter about arts students and their time to lounge around drinking coffee.

The plan is to meet Ciarán, but then as I'm heading out, Alice wanders past looking like a forlorn little lamb and I grab her arm.

"Oh, hi," she says, and bursts into tears.

Oh lord. Right.

I hug her for a bit and, holding the phone in my right hand, text Ciarán to tell him I've just run into a crying little sister and might be a bit late.

"What happened?" I ask. I haven't seen her like this since that eejit Eoin dumped her. She cries for a bit more, and something occurs to me. "I thought you were working today."

"Oh. Right. Yeah. I." And more tears.

Ciarán, because he is the best boyfriend ever, thank you oh good lord, texts back to say it's fine and to give Alice a hug from me. A definite keeper, that one.

"Here, you know what you need?" I pull out my smokes and offer her one.

"Oh, no, I –" She waves her hands about.

"Go on," I say, lighting one up for myself. "You'll feel better." All right, so maybe that's also why it's handy to have an outdoors job where it's easier to slip off and have a smoke. None of us are perfect.

"Yeah, all right then," she says.

We lean against the gates of college, puffing away. It's like old times, like two years ago, after I did my Leaving, the whole reason I started smoking in the first place, and we'd sit out in the garden smoking and talking about the future and our crazy relatives and that sort of thing. She gave up after her friend Lynn gave her this big lecture on the dangers of smoking, as though Alice is thick or something. Oh, dangerous, hadn't heard that before. Like everything else in the universe is so safe.

She's actually getting calmer by the minute, you can see it.

"Better?" I ask.

She nods, sniffles, dries her eyes. "Yeah. Thanks. Listen, don't tell Mum and Dad I wasn't at work, okay?"

I shrug. "Okay, whatever." As though they'd care that she's skiving off a single day in her summer job. She even drags herself into school when she's feeling sick, and she did Transition Year, for God's sake, and it's not like they do anything important at any point during the year anyway. "You sure you're going to be all right? Want to come for lunch with me and Ciarán?" Ah, I have to ask her. Even though I'm hoping she'll say no and let me off the hook.

"No, it's okay, I'm meeting Lynn soon," she says,

and then she smiles. "You're meeting Ciarán for lunch, huh?"

Right, so this is the part where she starts being my annoying sister again and I want to get rid of her. "Go. Go meet the Lynn-beast. I'll see you at home."

I'll have to buy chewing gum on the way, so that I don't get the speech about how he won't kiss anyone with ashtray-mouth from Ciarán. I light up another one, just one more, as I wait at the pedestrian crossing.

Of course they're bad for you. It's not like cigarettes are the only way to be self-destructive, though. My theory is that we all do it, in one way or another, and frankly I'd rather take my chances with the cancer sticks than throw myself into a screwed-up relationship or something. At least with these, you know what you're getting yourself into.

37

Chloe

Summer funerals just feel wrong. I imagine it must be so much easier to hang around graveyards watching boxes being lowered into the ground on days when it is wet and miserable and grey. Almost every other day this summer has been depressingly wintry. It figures that today would be the day the sun blasts down on us and reminds us that we're all wearing the worst colour to wear in this kind of heat.

And all the relatives keep saying is what great weather it is and aren't we lucky to have such a nice day for this.

I am going to go insane. I'm going to start shrieking and screaming, for all the wrong reasons.

Not out of grief, just out of frustration. Out of something I can't even identify.

Off we go to eat sandwiches with the crusts cut off and drink tea and beer or whatever it is the adults are drinking. It's at this hotel out near the graveyard. I wonder if they get a lot of this sort of business, post-funeral receptions. It must be depressing to have something like a Debs or a wedding reception here and then return here when someone you know dies.

"Just a fizzy water for me," Mam says to one of her sisters.

"Chloe, pet, do you want anything? Glass of wine?" Half my relatives think I'm barely out of secondary school. The other half are asking me what I'm doing in college or whether I'm working now, and what I'm having to drink.

I accept the glass of wine from my aunt because it's hit me again why Mam is having a fizzy water.

Everyone is just talking so normally and catching up with each other. My uncles are discussing cars and holidays.

I smile and answer questions about school and plans for the future. I am an actress, playing someone normal, or maybe a doll, with a painted smile and an empty head, or maybe me, all the time, pretending, and *I need to get out of here.*

38

Lynn

We are sitting down on the grass in St Stephen's Green, ice-cream cones in hand, by the time Alice explains what's going on.

"I quit my job," she says. "I actually just – just walked out of there. I can't – I just –"

"Why? What happened?" I was rather under the impression that everything was going fine there.

"Just – my supervisor was – oh, gosh, it's stupid, it's, I don't even *know*, and my parents are going to *kill* me, and I signed a contract with them, can you even quit if you sign a contract?" She looks at me like a lost puppy. "I'm going to be in so much trouble."

"No, you won't, you'll be fine," I say, half-laughing.

"You always say that," she says.

"You always worry too much." I catch the melting strawberry ice cream drips with my tongue. I love ice cream in the summer, and the winter too, if I'm honest, but there's something special about sitting outside on the grass with an ice-cream cone. "Alice. Seriously. It's going to be fine."

"It's *not* going to be fine," she snaps back at me. "I mean, they have my personal information, and what if I need a reference or something, and you're supposed to give in your notice, and, oh shit!" She draws her knees up to her chest and rests her chin on them, alternating biting at her nails with slurping at her ice-cream cone.

"Hey, don't bite your nails," I say, pulling her hand away.

"Don't tell me what to do," she says. She sounds cross, cranky, not like Alice.

I am rising above this. I am going to be understanding.

"Did something happen at work?" I ask.

She shrugs. "No. Yes. I don't know. I shouldn't have done it, I'm not – I'm not a quitter."

"Except for smoking," I say, trying to lighten the mood; maybe all she needs to do is laugh. She doesn't. Actually, she looks vaguely guilty.

Oh, for God's sake, I knew there was something

different-yet-familiar about her today. "Alice, you didn't."

"Yeah, one cigarette's really going to kill me."

"It's bad for you, and it's addictive, and . . ." I sigh. Why is it always so obvious to you when someone's doing something so stupid, why do you have to explain it in great detail to them? "Look, you know you shouldn't be smoking. You put so much effort into giving up."

"One cigarette. One. Calm down."

"I'm perfectly calm, you're the one who needs to calm down."

"I'm fine," she hisses.

I could use some of Mum's relaxation techniques right about now. It's not that I can't see that she's in some kind of bad mood, but it's hard to have sympathy for someone if they don't tell you why. This job thing is not the end of the world. It's a summer job, big deal. All that stuff about giving in notice – as though they care, in a place like that.

I sit and eat my ice cream and wait for Alice to return to her usual self. What is wrong with people this summer? Neil, and now Alice, turning into people I don't want to be around, people I don't feel comfortable with. And Simon's party.

I should have gone to that thing Sheila's doing. A new experience, a new location, a new set of skills, a new set of friends. Being kept busy and distracted. Having fun. Not having time to sit around feeling sorry for myself.

"Right," I say after we've been in sitting in silence for far too long and my ice cream is finished. I look over at Alice. She's still folded into herself, fiddling with the silver chain around her neck. "Oh, come on, stop worrying, it'll be *fine*." Maybe a little impatiently. I'm only human.

She takes a breath like she's going to say something important. "You always say that," she says in this little voice. "It's going to be fine. It's not. It's not always fine."

"Well, come on, it's not usually as bad as you think –"

"You said that when I was worried about Eoin, remember? I was all, oh, how can he like me, there's nothing special about me, and there *isn't*, and it is not *fine*, it's . . ." Her hands move, searching for the right word.

"Hey. Come on," I say. "It's time to get over Eoin. He's not worth it." Which is something so patently obvious that I shouldn't even have to say it. They broke up months ago.

And. Well. At least she had a chance with the boy she liked. At least they had an actual relationship.

"Is it? Is it really time to get over him?" she asks. Sarcastic. Cold.

"Long overdue, actually." Right back at you, newly bitchy Alice.

"You know," she says, scrambling to her feet, "you don't even – I mean, you've never even had a boyfriend. I don't know why I bother – I just –" And she's stormed off before I have a chance to get up.

There are two kinds of people in the world: the ones who run after huffy people and comfort them and give them all the attention they want, and the ones who don't let themselves get sucked into that dramatic posturing. Fine, Alice. Be like that.

I stay on the grass, watching people go by. Fine. Everything is just fine.

39

Alice

She doesn't follow me.

I don't know what I expected.

I don't know what I'm doing.

I'm angry, mostly. I can't talk to Jack about quitting because he'll tell our parents and they'll be angry or worse, disappointed. I can't talk to Lynn about it because she doesn't get it, and because she keeps saying everything's going to be fine as though it really will and as though my feelings don't count for anything and I hate that she always thinks she's right I hate it I hate it.

I was right, I was right when I wondered how on earth Eoin could have liked me, because he couldn't have, and he didn't, he didn't.

Chloe, perfect Chloe, little perfect beautiful always-knowing-what-to-say Chloe, and I didn't see it, and I am such an idiot.

I am so tired of being the one that people tell what to do, or yell at, or manipulate, or lie to. Good little Alice. Nice, sweet, kind. It's all such crap. I am not nice. I don't want to be nice. I want to scream at people. I want to hit them. I want big dramatic gestures.

And I don't know how to make big dramatic gestures happen. So I wait for the bus, and imagine how things with Lynn should have gone. Listening, not judging, sympathy and hugs and understanding that it's not just the job, it's everything, it's Eoin and Chloe, it's Chloe, it's me, it's who I am.

But then she's part of that. We don't have arguments. Because I won't argue with her, not really. Because it's not worth it. Because she always thinks she's right. Because I hate arguing.

I don't know why. It's strangely exhilarating, just storming off, just letting yourself be pissed off. You feel like you can do anything, if only you knew what exactly you wanted to do.

40

Chloe

I know it's a mistake from the moment I open my mouth but I have to say it anyway.

"So, Mam," I say, conversational, chatty, knowing that other people can hear, knowing that we have just buried her mother, knowing all of this and not caring because I have had two glasses of wine and maybe I am just a little upset. "Tell me now, why, exactly, do you keep having kids when you can't love them?"

Only maybe it comes out with a few more gulps and a few more tears than it sounds in my head.

I wonder for a second, when she looks at me, if she has asked herself the same question.

And then it comes, for the second time today, the slap across the face.

I know that anyone listening probably thinks I deserve it.

I bet they half-agree with my question, though.

I start running, crying, gasping for breath. Outside the sun is still shining. What a joke.

I don't know where to go.

There's a hand on my shoulder. Not Mam. Of course it isn't. Of course not.

"Come on, I'm going to take you home," Martin says.

"I'm not going to apologise to her," I say. "I'm not. I can't."

He sighs. "In the car. Now. You're going to go home and calm down, all right?"

"She hates me," I say, following him to the car.

He doesn't say anything, which must mean that it's true, but maybe I've known this all along and I've only been kidding myself.

Martin turns on the radio, maybe to stop me from saying anything else. He listens intently to the traffic report. "I'll go through town," he says to me. "Traffic's horrendous on the motorway."

I say nothing. I stay quiet and numb until we are in the middle of city centre traffic, waiting for the lights to turn green, and then I see someone in the sea of pedestrians.

"I'm going to get out here," I say to Martin.

"Don't be –" he starts to say, but I'm out of the car already, slamming the door behind me.

41

Neil

The last time I had a real conversation with Chloe was five years ago, which is sort of sad considering we were best friends almost all the way through primary school.

The version I told Lynn, who's sort-of friends with Chloe now, her friend Alice is Chloe's best friend, is that Chloe's the only girl I've ever kissed, which isn't even true, because the kiss didn't actually happen. It almost happened.

But it's a better first kiss story than your first kiss being with some random guy at a party when you're fifteen and drunk and don't even know his name. There was a history with Chloe, at least.

The truth is that Chloe is the sort of pretty that

makes you realise that if you don't really want to kiss her apart from trying to make her feel better when she's upset, because you think it might be the only thing that will work, there's definitely something going on.

"Hi, Neil, how's it going?" That's what she says to me. We're in the middle of town, and I'm supposed to be meeting Lynn in ten minutes, and she's just appeared out of nowhere and grabbed my arm.

"Hi," I say uncertainly. I have no idea what's going on. Years of avoiding each other in the corridors at school and now she's acting like we're best friends and nothing happened.

She walks along with me for a while, playing with her hair in that way that straight guys probably find hot. "So how are you?"

"Grand." I realise I have nothing to say to her. I'm not that great with new people. It takes a while before you figure out what you have in common and what you can laugh at together. And she's like a new person. Like a stranger. "What's up?"

"I just wanted to see you," she says, biting her lower lip. Another of her moves that's totally lost on me.

"Right." Trying to sound neutral. "How are things?" I look at her. Red eyes. She's been crying or drinking or both.

185

"It was my grandmother's funeral today," she says.

Because that's the sort of thing you tell someone you haven't been friends with in years.

"I'm sorry," I say as we turn off the street into Temple Bar, because what else can you say? I don't know what the right words are. I've never known anyone who died, not really. And what else can you say to someone you don't even know anymore?

She looks at me with big eyes. "I just thought that –" And then she starts over. "You were there for me, when my grandfather died, and I just thought –"

Is that how she remembers it? I was there for her? She cried, and I tried to kiss her, and she laughed in a hysterical sort of way and then ran off, and whenever I tried to talk to her about it she didn't want to, like she'd had enough of the subject already. I guess it was sort of messed up. We were kids. I didn't know what to say then and I don't know what to say now. We stopped talking to each other. I mean, it's impossible to stay friends with someone who lets you in and then shuts you out. Who has the patience for it, especially at eleven, for God's sake?

"That was years ago," I finally say. We're different people now.

It's like she's not even listening. "You were my

first real boyfriend, you know – you know me, you get me . . ."

We're coming up to the IFI, and I pause just before the entrance, looking at her. I have to sort things out with Lynn before Adrian arrives. And then Adrian's going to be here, and –

"I don't have time for this." I don't mean it to sound as cruel as it does. She's just lost another grandparent, and I don't understand death and what it does to you, I get that. But we're not friends. We haven't been friends for a long time. There's so much she doesn't know about me now.

She stares at me. "Oh."

Brilliant timing. Lynn is walking up just as Chloe starts crying. It's noisy and attention-grabbing. I can see passers-by looking on curiously. They probably think I've just dumped her or something.

I expect Lynn to hug her or something. Girls are experts at that. But instead she just stands next to us, arms folded.

"What did you do to her?" she finally asks me.

I can't tell if she's serious or not.

"Nothing," Chloe says. "Nothing." She dries her eyes. "Sorry, Lynn, he's all yours, I'm going to go." She disappears down the street before either of us has a chance to respond. She's insane. She is actually insane.

"What was that all about?" Lynn wants to know.

I shrug. "I have no idea. Now, my dear Miss Delaney, are we having coffee or what?" I'm hoping to get away from the topic of Chloe. Today's segment of our story doesn't exactly leave me looking like the good guy.

42

Lynn

"I didn't know you were still friends with Chloe," I say to Neil as we head inside for coffee. Friends or something else? I know it's a stupid question to even think. He and Adrian have whatever it is they have. I was there. But she's the girl, the girl he kissed, the girl of his childhood, and –

Well. Yeah. I'm jealous. This is what Neil has done to me. I am now the kind of girl who gets jealous of people.

He sighs. "I'm not. I just ran into her there." He's lying. I am sure of it.

"Okay," I say. "I give up."

He laughs, and then frowns. "What are you talking about?"

"I give up. Just stop lying to me, okay?"

"When did I lie to you?" He stops just before we go in the main doors and stares at me.

Well, if he's not going to admit the Chloe thing, then – "Adrian. Adrian's not gay? And then making me stay."

"Hey, I didn't *make* you do anything –"

"Oh, that is such crap." How can he really believe that? "God, you knew. You knew you could ask me to do anything, to be your little chaperone, make things easier for you, whatever, you knew I'd do it for you. So manipulative."

"Look, I didn't know that Adrian –"

"That's so not the point!"

"You know, you haven't even said that you're happy for me," he says.

We stand there and look at each other for a moment. Then the ground. Safer.

"I'm not," I say to the ground. "And you *know* why."

I can't look up. I can't look at him. This is the most humiliating thing I have ever had to do, admitting my stupidity here. What does he think of me now?

After an agonising pause, he says, "Why?"

I can't tell whether he's genuinely clueless or if he's letting me off the hook or if he just wants to hear me say it to stroke his ego. And before Adrian came along, I would have known. I would have been able to tell.

"Think about it," I say in exasperation, and turn on my heel and walk out.

It's not like what Alice did earlier. It's not storming off. It isn't.

Well, maybe. Just a little.

43

Alice

I am taking charge of my life. I am writing it down, putting it into words, making it real. I am venting. Once it is out there in the open, then everything will be okay. Then everything can go back to the way it used to be.

I type and I type and I type and the funny thing is that the more I do, the angrier I get. This is not how it is supposed to work. I am supposed to feel light and airy, as though a weight has been lifted from my shoulders, and instead it is getting heavier and heavier. It is crushing me.

What good is it to be angry with people if they don't know that you're angry at them? Isn't the whole point that I am sick and tired of being docile little Alice who lets people screw her over?

I log into my email account and instant messenger, and maybe there is too much of me left that is still timid Alice, little girl Alice, who doesn't want people to hate her. I have never wanted anyone to hate me. I just want them to know that what they're doing is wrong, that they are thoughtless and careless people.

New email account. I use a fake name, fake address. For now I am someone else. I think about my favourite television programmes when I pick my name. I become Serena Sawyer, my first name from *Gossip Girl* and my surname from *One Tree Hill*. I imagine I am beautiful and confident and entitled to tell people what I think of them.

And then I begin typing, copy-and-pasting, ranting again. Once I start I can't stop. I send messages to Lynn, to Eoin, and then to Erica for being gossipy and self-absorbed, to a couple of Eoin's friends, just because I would like them to know that they need to treat people as though they are real people.

And then Chloe. The Chloe messages are funny, because I log in to my instant messenger using my fake name, and add her email address, just to see, maybe, or just wanting to wait until she gets online and do it all as close to real time as possible, and within a few minutes she is online, and has added me back.

I tell her exactly what I think of her, in ugly words, and by the end of it I am crying.

Maybe she's gone away from the computer for a while, because I keep sending these truths that are spilling out of me, and it would take one click to block me, to stop reading them. And she doesn't. I type and type until I have nothing more to say, and then I go to mop up my eyes and tell my parents that I've quit my job.

44

Chloe

My phone is switched off so that Martin or Mam can't ring me, not that the latter would want to anyway, and the former has probably given up on me at this point. He's not at home by the time I get back. Gone back to Mam and everyone else, I suppose.

The Boy, I need to be with the Boy, I need to stop feeling this horrible and worthless and oh God, *Neil*, what on earth was I thinking?

This must be what it feels like to go crazy.

I am seeing if he is online when a Serena somebody adds me, and I click 'accept' almost automatically, even though I don't know any Serenas.

The messages are pouring in before I really know what's going on. I am logging on to other websites, seeing if I can get in touch with him this way or whether I will have to brave turning my phone back on, and it takes a few minutes to realise that I am being bombarded.

I am a bitch, selfish, a bad friend, manipulative, devious, ungrateful, a whore. Beautiful on the outside and hideous on the inside. After a while it all starts to melt together. I can't stop looking at the words.

It is not Steve. Not this time. The spelling is better.

I have no idea who it might be. It could be Neil, or Lynn, or any of my relatives, or any of my ex-boyfriends, or anyone, anyone at all. There are so many people it might be.

And then I'm laughing. I have to laugh. There are so many people it might be. It could even be my mother.

There is only one person I am sure it isn't.

I save the messages, when whoever this person is has finished, and then I go upstairs and throw a few things into a bag. What do I need? What do I not care about leaving behind? Underwear, some clothes, money. I am not sentimental. I just need to go, to get out of here, to be gone.

45

Eoin

In fairness, it was one kiss and I broke up with Alice almost straight away because I knew I was more into Chloe. And maybe I should have told her, but I didn't want to hurt her. Alice gets upset so easily. She shouldn't even care anymore. It's been so long. She should have moved on by now. Jesus. I can't believe she hung up on me.

Okay, maybe that was fair enough, actually.

Chloe's phone is still off. My patience might be wearing thin at this stage. Yes, she's gorgeous. Yes, she's amazing. But how much of this shit can one person take?

The doorbell rings, twice, before I realise I'm the only one at home. Parents are out having dinner, probably consoling each other about what a disappointment their son is or whatever, and Shelley's out with her friends.

She has a bag with her, a real bag, not those teeny-tiny girly handbags. "Moving in?" I ask.

She steps inside, kisses me, presses herself up against me. "I had a brilliant idea," she murmurs in my ear.

I think she's had that brilliant idea before, but I play along. "What is it?"

"Let's go somewhere. Wherever. Let's just get out of here."

"Like where?"

"I don't know! Somewhere. Just – away. You and me. Come on. You can get away from your dad, and we can just be together, don't you want that?"

For a second I even contemplate it. Then I look at the bag, listen to what she's saying. She keeps running her fingers over me, anywhere there's skin showing. She's fucking serious.

"We're a bit old for running away, aren't we?" I say, trying to make a joke out of it.

She turns cold straight away. "And you're a bit old for whining about your dad all the time, aren't you?" And then back to hot, nibbling on my neck. "Come on, just come with me. Please. You're the only one who actually cares about me."

"Hey, that's not true," I say.

She looks at me. "It is. It really is. You have no idea."

"Okay. So tell me." I nudge her away, stand out of reach, out of danger, and I wait for her to start talking. Tell me something. Anything.

"I can't," she finally says. "It's nothing."

How can I be the only one who actually cares about her, apparently, if she won't fucking *tell* me anything?

"I don't think this is working out." I hear myself saying it, and immediately I'm thinking, what, are you insane?

I look at her blinking back tears, and I'm going, oh don't cry, please don't cry, I'm going to feel like such a bastard, and then she puts her face in her hands and starts laughing, scarily.

"You're right. You're so right. I am so like my mother. I can't talk to you. I can't talk to anyone. I can't –" And then she's crying.

I've no idea what I'm supposed to do here. So I end up sitting down with her on the couch, letting her cry into my shoulder for a while, and then she switches her phone back on and calls her mum to come and pick her up.

I haven't met her mum before. She looks young but stressed out. You can see where Chloe gets her looks from, though.

"Thanks for minding my daughter for me," she says, half-smiling, mum-like. She puts a hand on Chloe's shoulder and my now ex-girlfriend flinches, like she's never had her mum do that before, and I watch them walk to the car, still kind of not sure what exactly just happened, but if I'm honest, glad that it's over.

Part Four

Back Again

46

Lynn

Even in sixth year, some of the teachers still tell you where to sit and who to sit next to, as though you're first-year babies all over again. We leap straight into things. No how-was-your-summer, easing gently back into the routine. My music teacher, Mrs Anderson, is pleased to hear that I got some practice in over the last month of the summer, but promptly sets a load of homework for us all anyway.

I got a letter in the post about being 'appointed' a prefect, which means I get to run around doing things for the first years, because I am now a responsible sixth year in need of time to fill, apparently.

You'd think I'd be kicking up a fuss about not really having a choice in the matter, but it looks good on a CV and it's good to have something to do. After Trish's workshop, I thought about auditioning for another orchestra or taking up another instrument or something along those lines, but I have enough going on between school and reintroducing myself to my violin and taking yoga classes. Classes with Trish, not Mum; they're a bit more energetic than what Mum does. More movement. It's almost like dancing. There's a mix between people close enough to my age and people of Mum's age, but everyone gets along rather than there being a line down the middle. It's good.

Already I can see that I'm going to spend my year hopping from one thing to another, and honestly I'm glad. It's familiar. I feel like I'm using my time well again.

In chemistry, our teacher puts me and Neil sitting together, even though I suppose that she thinks she's being nice to us, seeing as we were lab partners last year.

"So," he says, putting his books down on the workbench next to mine.

"So," I say, looking at him. There's something different about him. Maybe it's the fact that I don't look at him and want to kiss him. "How's Adrian?" I ask, more out of something to say than out of any real curiosity.

He shrugs. "He's okay."

"You don't sound very enthusiastic."

"It's not new anymore," he says. "You know what I mean?"

"Sure," I say. "You're totally bored of him." I laugh to show him that I'm only joking.

He grins back. "Totally, you have no idea. I only keep him around for the sex. Now you, my dear Lynn, how have you been?"

And just like that, we're friends again.

Or maybe real friends for the first time.

47

Alice

Lynn half-smiles at me as I pass her by in the corridor, which is something.

First days back always make me nervous. This one in particular, because I am walking into school on my own, and it is a return to exams and proper subjects and academic madness. We have been sorted into new groups for English, Irish and maths; there are people I've never had a class with before, some who've just come straight from third year, in my other subjects. French, history, biology, art. One of Eoin's friends is in my art class, and in our first class, he keeps looking at me as though there's something strange about me, as though my uniform jumper is inside-out or my hair's sticking up oddly or something.

"He's so into you," Donna laughs when I tell her on our way to lunch. Lunch scares me, the thought of sitting alone and having no one to talk to, but we have history together before lunch on this first day and it's easier than it might otherwise be just to walk along with her and sit down in the canteen as though I belong there.

"He is not," I say, but the way she says it makes it sound like a fact.

"Hey, what's the story with Chloe?" John, Donna's boyfriend, wants to know, as he and a couple of other people from our year join us.

"Heard she pulled a Dominic," one of John's friends says.

Donna puts her face in her hands. "Oh my God, that is so tasteless."

"She just switched schools," I volunteer. The way I say it makes it sound as though we are still friends, when actually Mum ran into Martin, Chloe's stepfather, at the supermarket. I was worried that I'd get into trouble for not being friends with Chloe anymore, or something, but it didn't even come up. It is strange the things you worry about that end up being nothing. No one yelled at me for quitting my job either. Mum and Dad didn't even seem disappointed in me, which would have been horrible, they just said something about it probably being best to be away from crazy supervisors and that hopefully I wouldn't end up working in a shop as a full-time job anyway. And then my day of crazy ranty emails. Right after, I started worrying about IP addresses being tracked, and people comparing notes and figuring out who had sent them, but after chatting to Jack and asking deliberately vague questions, I realised that half of them would have gone straight into spam folders anyway. And the rest – ignored, I guess, dismissed as lunacy. Which is what they were, really.

'Serena' sent an apology to Chloe straight after I heard that she was switching schools, which, if Martin mentioned he'd been talking to my mother, probably makes it very obvious that it was me. I think I can live with that, though, if I ever run into her again and we talk about it.

It was a silly thing to do. I deleted the account straight after sending Chloe that apology. I am the kind of girl who can walk out on jobs. I should be able to tell people to their faces if I have a problem with them. It's just so hard, sometimes, to find the right words on the spot, to get it all out without stammering or blushing or running away.

"Probably wanted to get away from all the silly rumours," Donna says. "I would have."

"Yeah, you're not interesting enough to talk about, though," John teases.

I laugh and go 'oooh' with the rest of them at the table.

When I looked in the mirror this morning I could see the difference: I am now much more of a swan than an ugly duckling. And for tiny moments, like this, sometimes I even feel it.

I just wish that it was as magical as it is in fantasies.

48

Chloe

Eoin sends me a text message saying that he hopes I'm doing okay, and that the latest story is that I left school because one of the teachers knocked me up. I crack up, especially because I'm at the doctor's with Mam. My new school doesn't start back for another couple of days, not for fifth years anyway, and Martin's back at work and Patrick's gone off to 'big school' looking so adorable you could cry, so I'm here.

She doesn't say thanks for coming, but she did ask me, so I suppose that's something.

"How are your sessions going?" she asks.

I shrug. "They're okay." I pause. "They use, you know, really clichéd phrases? Like 'inner child'. She actually said that to me once."

And she was kidding, but it is a good story, something to tell Mam. "You're not serious."

"Any day now, she's going to tell me to chase after my own personal rainbow. I can't wait." I giggle and Mam laughs with me.

On the one hand I find the whole notion of counselling ridiculous. It's talking to a complete stranger about your feelings and your personal life. On the other hand, it's talking to a complete stranger about your feelings and your personal life. They really are just there to listen.

I'm finding words for things. I'm looking at my behaviour a lot. It is entirely self-indulgent, but in a guilt-free sort of way.

I am never going to have the warm fuzzy mother who'll stroke my hair and talk to me about boys, but at least I can have this, sitting here waiting for her to get to see how my new little brother or sister is doing.

I am hoping for a little sister, because I already have the wonderful little brother, and I want a little girl around the place so I can tell her she's beautiful, so that she hears it from someone other than boys and doesn't feel like she owes them something or that it's not really true.

And I'll tell her that she shouldn't worry about breaking hearts, and just focus on her own first of all, because that's really what you're doing anyway, making sure you don't get hurt, and I will hug her every day, to remind her that she is loved.

The doctor calls Mam in, and I sit and wait to find out what the future has in store for us all.

The End.

Also published by poolbeg.com

BIG PICTURE

Claire Hennessy

There's more to life than exams.
Except when it's the Leaving Cert.

Sixth year. It's the year of: crazy studying,
frantic calculations of points, and putting your life on
hold for the sake of your future. So Vicky
and Anna have always believed, anyway.

It is most certainly not a year of: developing an addiction to
bad reality television, trying to have a relationship with a
boy who doesn't believe in 'being serious', becoming
hopelessly infatuated with a college student, suddenly not
having a clue what you want to do with the rest of your life,
fights with your best friends, uncovering secrets in your
family, contemplating what being 'smart' really means,
and finding any excuse to have a party – right?

ISBN 978-1-84223-317-7

Also published by poolbeg.com

that
girl

Claire Hennessy

Kim's not the kind of girl who worries too much,
but there's something about her upcoming 16th birthday
celebration that's stressing her out.

Is it her anxiety about mixing friends who haven't met
before? Is it that one person after another is dropping out to
go to a concert instead? Or the fear that her parents will
hover over everyone all night long? Or could it be her
confused feelings about her brother's friend, someone she's
known since she was a kid and who understands her the
way very few people do? Is there any place for such a
friendship in her life? Shouldn't her great boyfriend
be enough?

Last time she checked, birthday parties were meant to be
fun – but this one is looking like a disaster waiting to happen!

*All the drama, all the insight, all the fun
that we have come to expect — her best novel to date!*

ISBN 978-1-84223-288-0